THE HAVE NOTS

Published by Lonely Whale Press

Astoria, Oregon

This is a work of fiction. All names, characters, places and incidents either are products of the author's imagination or are used fictitiously. No reference to any real person is intended or should be inferred.

Cover and Interior Design by We Got You Covered Book Design

ISBN: 979-8-9886295-2-8

THE HAVE NOTS

A NOVEL

WILLIAM DEAN

FOR MY SONS,
JESSE AND JACOB

CONTENTS

"HE IS A FRIEND OF THE POOR AND THE WEAK,
AND AN ENEMY OF THE PROUD AND CRUEL."

THE MERRY ADVENTURES
OF ROBIN HOOD

1883

———

"HE TURNED THE POWER TO THE HAVE-NOTS.
AND THEN CAME THE SHOT."

RAGE AGAINST THE MACHINE

1992

PART 1

THE CHOSEN ONE

CHAPTER
ONE

A KILLER HANGOVER was out there, lurking like a villain in the impenetrable darkness, the shadow of night. Waiting to jump out and clobber.

Just as the man sitting alone at the bar had hoped.

He'd been pounding down doubles since mid-afternoon, and it was now nearing closing time. He didn't know the name of the joint. Didn't care. Hours earlier, he'd stumbled out of another nameless dive and ended up at this slimehole. Wherever the hell it was.

When the bartender approached warily, Jeremy Devon Stone was well on his way to passing out or puking. Quite possibly both.

The stooped man on the stool resembled just another sloppy drunk. Stone, however, had a plan and was executing it masterfully. With every shot of bottom shelf whiskey, he was that much closer to forgetting The Call. With every gulp, remembering what was said seemed less likely, and that was a good thing. A very good thing.

The ponytailed barkeep at MacDougal's, a dingy south side watering hole popular with construction workers and hockey fans, didn't know Stone. He was too dressed up to be a regular, with his gray wool sport coat, collared white shirt and black jeans. No, this guy wasn't part of the usual clientele in their unwashed flannel and frayed ballcaps, shouting over their beer.

Stone's eyes were shut, and the bartender paused to look him up and down. Late 20s. No wedding ring. Expensive haircut. Day's worth of stubble on his chin.

Within reach on the scratched mahogany bar, a long, narrow notebook rested. There were scribbles on the cover. Many of the inside pages were dog-eared. A journalist on a bender most likely, the toweled man thought.

He reached across and tapped the stranger's arm, bent around an empty rocks glass.

"Hey, man."

Stone's eyes fluttered open, blue and red creating a new disturbing color. He straightened and immediately belched. His breath was foul.

Catching a whiff, the bartender winced.

"Rough day?"

"You could say that."

"How many drinks you had?"

"Not enough."

"You don't know?"

"Know what?"

"How many drinks. You've been here all night."

"Fuck's sake. Didn't know I was s'posed to count."

The bartender stood silently for a moment, wondering if he should give this dude the boot. Or show a little kindness and call a cab.

"Since yer jus' standing there, how 'bout another whiskey?" Stone said, pushing his luck – if he had any left to push. The words came out slurred and drenched in spittle.

The man behind the bar scowled, but moments later turned on his heels and grabbed the bottle. He poured another gut-grinding double but didn't release the glass until he made firm eye contact with Stone.

"Last call," he growled. "You're done."

Stone grunted and immediately chugged the drink, wiping his mouth with the sleeve of his coat. He tossed two crisp fifties on the bar, stuffed the notebook in his back pocket and stumbled out into the rain.

Cursing and mumbling like a crazy person, he managed to order an Uber after several clumsy fails. Despite his obvious impairment, he'd have tried to drive home – if he could remember where he parked. He thought he'd walked up a hill to reach the bar with no name, but that part was pretty hazy.

Key chunks of memory were already failing, like a building shivering before its collapse. It would only get worse, he knew. His plan was working brilliantly.

He looked up at the ceiling of clouds, stuck out his tongue and felt the tickle of raindrops. He smiled in a lopsided way. A deliriously defiant way.

It was the worst day of his life. Check that: *One* of the worst days. But with any luck, he wouldn't remember a thing tomorrow.

Not a goddamn thing.

———

The first call came at 6:45 a.m., followed by another at 7:14. The third try to reach him was recorded at 8:08. The fourth at 8:29.

The fifth attempt, causing his vibrating cell phone to once again dance atop the nightstand, finally caught his attention.

Slowly rolling over and pulling himself onto his elbows, movements that required considerable effort, Stone checked the small screen, taking a few moments to focus. It was 9:20. His head was throbbing mercilessly. He noticed he was still wearing his jeans and button-down shirt.

He had no idea where he'd been. The only certainty was that alcohol was involved. He crawled out of bed and shuffled to the bathroom. There were streaks of vomit in the sink, a clue to a mystery that would never be solved.

Glancing at the mirror, he recoiled, seeing a man far older and more haggard than himself. Shaking out a half-dozen extra-strength Tylenols, he downed them all without water. It wouldn't be enough to stop the throbbing, but he'd at least be able to summon the strength to take another look at his phone.

Stone sat on the edge of the bed, feeling sick. There were 13 new voicemails, five from this morning alone. And every damn one of them was from work.

He groaned. While he couldn't remember much of the previous night, God was apparently playing a cruel trick. Most of his memory of The Call hadn't been erased after all. It came back to him with a jolt when he played the first message.

It was from his editor, the long-suffering Sally Betters.

"Jeremy, this is Sally. Sorry to call you so early, but I wanted to remind you about the meeting today with the ME. Don't be late."

The next calls were increasingly frantic. "Don't forget the meeting, Jeremy. It's very important. Pick up your damn phone!"

The most recent call sounded angry.

"The ME just messaged me, asking where the hell you are. You're really digging yourself a deep, deep hole, Jeremy. If it's even possible to dig any deeper. Like I said yesterday, this is your last chance to tell your side of the story. Plead for mercy or whatever. Save your effed-up career if you can. But you can't even get that right, can you? Out drinking all night again? Jesus. I can't believe you're making me do this. Well, I'm not rushing over there to save your sorry ass this time. Get over here pronto, or you're going to really regret it. It's your last chance."

Stone grimaced, feeling a measure of regret for having put his editor in this position. During the toughest days, with the libel suit and all the fallout, she'd been his most vocal defender. Earlier, when his wife died and the drinking got worse, Betters quietly arranged to get him some time off – even check him into a clinic. She was his fact-checker, his last line of defense, his champion, his savior.

Until yesterday. That's when everything changed. That's when he knew he'd be fired. And a journalist fired for screwing up has no future. Not in journalism anyway.

Bleary-eyed, he shed his clothes and stumbled into the shower, drenching himself with cold water. There was a near-empty fifth of Southern Comfort next to the shampoo and the sight of the bottle in such an unlikely place made him cry. Long, heaving sobs that only made his head hurt more.

As water streamed down his face, he considered taking the elevator to the top of the Tudor Arms and jumping off.

Fly, baby, fly.

But he couldn't do it, he knew. He lacked his late wife's courage – her brave and resolute desire to control the timing of her final breaths. He lacked a lot of things, all of which had become tragically obvious.

Besides, his editor deserved better. She'd no doubt blame herself for his suicide, for failing to prevent it from happening, and that was something he couldn't bear. Not after burying the woman he loved.

Not after running from her pain and torment.

He'd never truly appreciated Betters until this moment, when he was about to get canned. When he was about to lose the last thing in his life that really meant something.

The last thing.

He popped a few more Tylenols and got dressed, choosing a blazer that didn't smell like sour whiskey. From the sidewalk outside the lobby, he hailed a cab. He still didn't know where his car was.

"Rough night?" the driver asked as they headed for the Chronicle building, about 14 blocks away.

"You could say that."

"It'll get better."

"Oh yeah? How do you know?"

"The odds are in your favor."

"I wouldn't bet on me," Stone groused. "Not today."

The Chronicle was one of those big city newspapers from a gilded age, one filled with Pulitzers, a sprawling and bustling newsroom, powerful investigative teams with seemingly unlimited resources, well-endowed overseas bureaus and a stable of columnists who appeared regularly on cable TV, musing about this or that.

Those days were long gone. The paper today was a distant cousin of its former self, with a quarter of the circulation and staff. The presses no longer rolled at midnight. There were none around to roll. That job had been farmed out to save money.

One could argue that the paper, while considerably downsized, hadn't let the quality of its day-to-day reportage slip, although the I-Team had long been disbanded and the once revelatory statehouse bureau slashed from eight reporters to an anemic two. Despite everything it had lost, despite the growing distance from the glory years, the Chronicle was still a relevant, interesting and occasionally hard-hitting information source. Or so Stone believed, fervently, in his heart.

He entered the newsroom and headed to the ME's office the most direct way possible – down a hallway adorned with prestigious awards mounted on plaques and poster-sized photographs snapped by staffers that captured some of the biggest news events the nation and world has known. The Great Depression. World War II. The Kennedy assassinations. Vietnam and the college protests. Watergate. The first Black president. The storming of the Capitol.

The hall was always awe-inspiring, but Stone couldn't look.

He approached David Burgess' glass-walled office with sweaty palms. The ME was behind his oversized, cluttered desk in his usual dark suit. Betters was sitting across from him, looking agitated.

Burgess spotted Stone and waved him in.

"You look like shit," the managing editor said. "I can guess why you didn't make our morning meeting."

Clearly frustrated, Betters frowned.

"Yeah, sorry," Stone said in a coarse whisper. "I wasn't exactly eager to meet my executioner."

"Executioner, huh? Well, if you were a cat, you'd be out of lives, that's for sure. I'm trying to figure out how such a talented reporter can go so astray. So off the rails. Sally seems to think it's the drinking. I'm thinking you just stopped giving a shit. That you want me to fire you out of some twisted sense of victimhood. Is that it?"

"Sally's right. It's the drinking. I'm … I'm not thinking straight."

Burgess shook his head, looking truly perplexed.

"You came here straight out of J-school at Columbia, top of your class. You quickly became one of our star reporters. We gave you the biggest stories, you *broke* some of the biggest stories. Your investigation into police corruption and payoffs put a dozen cops in jail. You won every damn award shy of a Pulitzer. Your reporting was thorough, rock solid. Always multiple sources backed up by hard evidence.

"And then, seemingly out of nowhere, the wheels started falling off. All the errors Sally caught in your copy, if they had gotten into print … and then that damn lawsuit. Quotes attributed to the wrong person? Even if it was an honest screwup, it's deeply troubling. I need to be able to trust my reporters – trust that they won't make mistakes that put us in hot water. Hard-nosed journalism is one thing, sloppy reporting and writing is another.

"Jeremy, I need to be completely honest. I don't trust you right now."

Stone felt tears welling. The last thing he wanted was to hurt the paper and the journalists who worked so hard every day, striving for excellence. He was falling apart, yes, but he never intended to bring anyone down with him.

Just the night before, he hid behind a bottle, hoping to avoid facing an ugly truth. Now he just wanted to get it over with. His forehead was damp but his mouth dry as dust. His head began throbbing again, like something vile was inside his brain, beating a drum.

"Fire me. I deserve it," he said, swallowing hard.

Burgess nodded.

"That's true. But I still haven't entirely given up on you," he said.

Stone could see Betters shaking her head, looking perturbed. Had she finally given up on her protégé?

"David, I thought we were going to, um, put an end to this," she said in a low voice. "For his sake as well as ours."

Burgess shrugged apologetically. "Yes, I know. That *was* my thinking, but I've had a change of heart. I only hope it doesn't bite me in the ass."

Furrowing his brows, he glowered at the reporter in front of him.

"Screw up again and you're finished," he said. "That's one more factual error. Toe the line and bust your butt. Break news like you used to do, but do it the right way. Stop drinking, cold turkey. Take a few days if you have to, then get your ass here and roll up your sleeves. Sally will be my eyes and ears, and know this: One single misstep and I will not hesitate to send you packing with my foot up your ass. Understood?"

"Yessir."

"Good. Now get the hell out of my office. You've wasted enough of my time today."

Stone left the room shaken, but in a good way. He felt the knot inside him loosen. No longer a condemned man, he suddenly felt like hitting the corner bar to celebrate and a split second later realized that wasn't a good idea. He needed to focus. Hunker down. Find the mojo that had abandoned him in his self-torment. And avoiding booze was the key.

He felt his phone vibrate and fished it out. The caller's name surprised him.

"This is Jeremy."

"Hello, my friend. How are you doing?"

"Things are finally looking up," Stone said, and for a change he meant it. At least he was still working. "How's the church, Father? Still running detox centers?"

"Oh yes, and much more," the caller said cheerfully. "Are you still handling big stories or have they sidelined you because of the lawsuit? Heard about the settlement. Costly, but at least it's over."

The libel suit was public knowledge – the tabloids had a field day – but the payout at the end was a secret. Supposedly.

Yet the caller knew. *Of course he did.*

It was amazing how connected he was, with sources across the city, from the inner sanctums of City Hall to the most squalid, drug-infested neighborhoods. There was a logical explanation, of course. When nobody else gave a crap about the homeless and their litany of problems, from mental illness and sexual abuse to addiction, the pastor stepped in to handle the dirty work, landing contracts worth millions.

People's Oasis Church now had a near monopoly on shelter beds and related support services, but that was dwarfed by the church's biggest endeavor – a network of detox centers that treated several thousand "unfortunate souls" every six months. A little-known secret was how many of the unfortunates came from rich families. Heroin spiked with fentanyl and overprescribed oxy were equal opportunity plagues.

Stone knew more than most about the religion-infused centers, because he recently had been a patient in one of them, thanks to his editor.

That's where he first met the Rev. Charles Immanuel Caprice, known to almost everyone, especially the people living on the streets, as simply Father.

"Nah, I'm still doing my job," Stone said, relieved to be uttering those words. "Why are you calling, Father?"

"I'm glad," he said gently, ignoring the question. "I've always thought highly of you. Our discussions were always enlightening. Langston thought so, too."

There was silence as Stone stepped to the window wall to make sure the call remained private. Caprice knew many of his innermost secrets, divulged during the treatment process as a form of healing. Or maybe just because the church was curious. He wondered where all that information went, whether it was being used in some way.

But maybe he was being his old paranoid self.

The reference to Langston struck him as odd.

Caprice's right-hand man, Langston was a craggy former cop who served as both an adviser and bodyguard. He shielded the preacher from gun-toting drug dealers and gang leaders who viewed his rise as a threat to their illicit business ventures. But Langston was never present when Stone was in treatment, revealing his troubles and fears.

"Jeremy, are you there?"

"Yes."

"Good. I have something for you, something very special," he said. "I suppose it's what you would call a big 'scoop.' Is that the right word?"

"Scoop, right. What's going on?" Stone was still too fuzzy-headed to be his usual perceptive self.

"I can't talk about it now, over the phone. We need to meet in person in a few days. Then you'll see."

"You're being awfully mysterious. Look, I've been going through a lot of things and, um, I don't know. … This may not be a good time."

The pastor chuckled. "You don't want to miss out on this, Jeremy. You'd never forgive yourself."

Stone rolled his eyes. How many times had he been promised a bombshell only to dig down to the root of a baseless conspiracy theory? How many times had he wasted weeks turning over rocks and tracking down elusive sources only to be bitterly disappointed?

Maybe he owed the caller something for pulling him off the ledge. A small favor perhaps. But he couldn't risk tumbling down rabbit holes. He needed to start knocking balls out of the friggin' park to get Betters, his newly designated probationary overseer, off his back.

"Why me? There are lots of reporters in this city."

"Ah, but you're the only one I really know."

Through the phone, Stone could hear the sound of heavy trucks rumbling and men shouting.

"I'm going to have to cut this short, I'm afraid," Father continued after a long moment. "I have some logistics to attend to. I'll text you the information. It was nice talking to you, Jeremy."

Stone shook his head, causing another wave of pain. He craved a shot of whiskey. Just to clear the lingering fog, put his thoughts in better order. But he couldn't, shouldn't, *wouldn't* risk another relapse. Not now, when he'd gotten an unexpected reprieve – a final crack at turning his miserable life around.

He walked over to the elevators wondering when the fog would lift. He squeezed his head between his hands but it didn't help.

"Fuck, fuck, fuck," he muttered as the stainless steel doors slid open, revealing a mother and young child. "Ooh, sorry."

Wide-eyed, they hurried away. Suddenly worried about his lack of impulse control, he stepped into the empty car and pressed the lobby button. Checking his phone, he saw that the pastor's text had already been sent:

Thursday 7 a.m., Turner Island. I'll be waiting for you at the first stop off the bridge. Don't be late! You don't want to miss this.

What the hell?

Turner Island was about the least likely spot to meet a man of the cloth, especially one who'd taken a vow of poverty. Just seven miles long and a brisk 40-minute walk from shore to shore at the narrowest point, the enclave was one of the wealthiest in the nation per capita.

A half-dozen billionaires had mansions there. Megamillionaires, too. Their yachts and helipads lined the south shore facing the estuary. The only way in or out was a two-lane state road on a floating bridge that extended about four miles from the mainland, functioning like an elongated cul de sac.

It's the route the work-a-day folks used to go back and forth to their island jobs, serving the rich. Time magazine once described the leafy bedroom retreat, with its appointment-only Louis Vuitton, Prada and Tiffany & Co. showrooms, as "the most decadent *nouveau riche* place on Earth."

Why would Caprice want to meet there?

His blistering sermons frequently chastened the One Percenters for failing to do more to help the downtrodden. Without a doubt, he was the city's fiercest critic of the ultra-rich, frequently giving well-attended lectures on the subject at local colleges.

Maybe he convinced one of the resident billionaires to donate to his church, Stone thought. Perhaps build a new shelter or two. More likely than not, the promised "scoop" was a PR event spurred by a tycoon eying a tax write-off.

Stone didn't write stories like that. His career had been built on bulldog reporting, capped with often unforgettable confrontational interviews. He'd exposed corrupt government officials, revealed hidden dangers and systemic failings that had saved lives. His awards didn't line the sacred corridor at the paper, but there were enough to fill a pair of large cardboard boxes currently taking up valuable closet space in his downtown apartment.

A fluff piece? No way.

Outside on the sidewalk, Stone passed the corner bar where he'd been hundreds of times – a favorite haunt of his colleagues called the M&M. Fortunately, he couldn't peek inside. The blinds on the grimy windows were permanently down.

There was a sandwich board in his path announcing happy hour deals. Half-off well drinks, $4 beers. He reflexively licked his lips but forced himself to keep moving. He had to find his car, and it would be easier to do that before dark.

He'd drive out to Turner Island as requested, he resolved. An hour max, then make up some excuse to leave. He owed the preacher that much at least.

Having a plan made him feel more at ease. He smiled despite himself. Despite the menace still swirling around him.

At least he was still working.

TWO

LANGSTON was a hard man to read. Some would say impossible.

He had dark, deep-set eyes and a creased leathery face that betrayed no hint of emotion or concern. He also stared, unblinking, for disturbingly long intervals.

And yet Father somehow always knew what Langston was thinking. Even feeling. And right now, the beefy former policeman was feeling nervous.

"The revolution has begun. The fuse is lit. There's no stopping it now," Father said, hanging his ceremonial robe. With his shining gold-flake eyes, medium beard and long brown hair parted down the middle, he looked like a Hollywood version of Jesus.

"*Our* revolution, my friend."

"Our revolution," Langston repeated, but in a robotic way, minus the pastor's lyrical tone.

"Is something troubling you?"

Hands clasped behind his back, Langston began pacing the small room behind the pulpit where the sermons were written – his footsteps thumping from his 250 pounds. It was a habit he'd picked up working murder cases. Sometimes walking around the corpse revealed things. Tiny pieces of evidence and other clues he might otherwise miss. Other times it was a way of distancing himself from the carnage and the stench. The horror of it all.

Father found the pacing amusing. A cartoon character with a lightbulb over his head.

"It's Stone," Langston said after a while. "Can he be trusted?"

"Yes, of course."

"Yeah, but word on the street is he's hitting the sauce again. *Hard.* He's about to get canned from that rag of his."

"I know," Father said. "That's why he's perfect. And that's why you were also perfect, my friend."

"I don't understand."

"Sure you do. You remember when we met, don't you? You were 'hitting the sauce' as you say, plus a few other substances. You'd lost your job in disgrace. You were contemplating suicide."

Langston bowed his head, revealing a patchy crew cut. "And you saved me."

"You saved yourself, I was merely playing my part. The point is, I couldn't have hoped for a better person to serve at my side. I have the same feeling about Stone. When the news breaks, he'll step up. He'll know what to do. Instinctively. We merely need to have him in the right position at the right time."

"But he's not the type to be loyal to anyone. We can't control him."

Father raised the simple, unadorned chalice he used for services and took a sip of red wine.

"That's where the photograph from your associate comes in," he told Langston, who'd finally stopped moving. "But only as a last resort. We must be careful to bend Stone to our purpose, but not break him. As we both know, he's of no use to anyone when broken. Besides, the adrenalin of the story will control him. It always does."

"If he bothers to show up. He'll probably be at the bottom of a bottle somewhere."

"He'll come. Have a little faith."

CHAPTER
THREE

BETTERS DIDN'T deserve this shit. Absolutely not.

As the paper's senior assistant managing editor, she was built to lead major projects and investigations. She'd be the one to win another news Pulitzer, ending the Chronicle's 27-year drought. She'd return the paper to greatness – if the top bosses would let her run her team with maximum support and minimal interference.

But she couldn't do it while Stone, her star player turned albatross, was pulling her down. How could she triumph while babysitting a drunkard? And now, just when the ME was about to cut him loose and set her free, Stone was given yet another chance.

Betters raised her no-frills gin and tonic and took a big gulp. From her seat at the M&M, she could see several reporters and low-level editors. She ignored their waves, preferring not to socialize with them.

As a woman rising out of one of the poorest neighborhoods in Baton Rouge, Betters was tough and uncompromising. While city editor of the college paper at LSU, she brought several students to tears, savagely critiquing their story drafts. When the faculty adviser brought her into his office to go over the complaints, she shrugged.

"I did them a favor," she said. "They're awful. They have no business going into journalism."

After graduation, Betters made a name for herself as a dogged reporter who could also write brilliantly – a rare combination. At the midpoint of her career, she reluctantly transitioned to editing, seeking better pay and shorter hours. Her friends dourly predicted that she'd hate the desk job, but she quickly proved to be a natural. She excelled as an editor in charge of young reporters hungering for success, or at least a shot at cracking the front page. Over time, she mellowed, turning down the heat on her edits and emerging as the paper's best mentor and writing coach.

The journalist she took the most pride in molding was Stone.

He arrived brash and confident beyond reason, but Betters knew right away that he had a gift. He could get the most reluctant and reclusive sources to talk on the record. Some he'd bully. Some he'd sweet talk. Whatever it took. The quotes would magically appear at the top of his stories, amazing the newsroom and stoking the envy of his rivals at the city's tabloids.

Betters took Stone under her wing, teaching him the finer points of story organization and a more polished writing style. He flourished, his byline soon becoming synonymous with a must-read story. Betters' best assignments began flowing his direction. As the eye-popping exclusives mounted, Stone became the Chronicle's golden boy, the first name mentioned at the editors' weekly planning meetings whenever a piece was pitched that required a tenacious and fearless reporter.

"Put Stone on it," Burgess often said. "He'll get it done."

Everything seemed to be working out beautifully until lightning struck Stone in the form of a diagnosis. Leukemia, advanced enough to start a countdown clock on his wife's life. Eight months left, possibly 12, the doctor said.

It would turn out to be nine months and 13 days, with Jenny becoming her own reaper. Her suicide, while not altogether surprising, devastated Stone, who had been coping with the illness, or more accurately avoiding dealing with it, by working even more hours at the paper.

In the end, he had returned home late one night to find the lights off as usual. He trudged up the stairs to the bedroom and saw his wife under the blankets. It wasn't until he climbed in bed next to her, finding her body oddly cold, that he noticed the empty bottle of sleeping pills and the note.

Apologizing for the inconvenience, she expressed her love in a way that brought Stone immediately to tears.

She didn't mention how he'd gone AWOL as a husband, how he'd drifted away to avoid being so close to death. The note said nothing about how she'd relied on her sister to take her to the hospital for treatment because he was never around – always on some deadline or another.

"I hope you find peace," she wrote instead, even though she was the one finally finding it. "Love always, Jenny."

Not a hint of bitterness or resentment. And that brought Stone to his knees.

Her suicide rocked him like nothing else could. It broke him in unimaginable ways – a web of cracks in a pane of glass that keeps on spreading. The more he dwelled on his misery, the more soul-crushing it became.

Stone tried to drink away the pain, and it seemed to work for a while. The numbing came courtesy of whiskey. The cheap stuff that came in a jug and seared your throat. Napalm in a glass.

Nobody was more acutely aware of Stone's headlong dive toward rock bottom than Betters, who performed the role of cranky mother figure in the drama.

She was in her 50s and no longer resisting the graying of her short afro. Straight and decidedly single, having found long-term relationships stifling, she held zero romantic interest in Stone yet had in her possession a key to his eighth-floor studio. It was the place he'd rented weeks after the funeral in hopes of pulling himself together – learning how to live beyond his guilt and grief. That, of course, proved impossible.

He'd initially handed over the front door key so she could feed his dwindling assortment of tropical fish and water a shaggy Boston fern named Marley when he was on the road, tracking people down. "Scooplets," he'd call the exclusive interviews.

The key came in handy when Stone started missing work and going radio silent. She'd find him sprawled on the bed or the floor, reeking of stale booze, and she'd drag him into the shower and turn on the water.

He had a Keurig in the kitchen but rarely any pods, so Betters took to sticking a few in her bag. A mug of steaming black coffee would be waiting when he stumbled out of the bathroom.

"You're too good to me," he'd say in a raspy voice.

"You're right," she'd reply, arms folded across her chest. "Get your shit together. I'm not your babysitter."

But she'd become exactly that.

It was a terrible thing, watching Stone deteriorate, piece by piece. Betters found herself covering for him more and more. When asked by higher-ups why a big story was taking so long, she'd tell them the documents needed to support the premise were delayed. Or key sources needed more convincing. There were plenty of fake excuses to draw from. A pile of them.

She hated deceiving her boss. Hated putting her job at risk even more. But she would have gone on doing it if Stone hadn't reached a new low. The libel suit.

It seemed to come out of nowhere, over a relatively modest gotcha story about $6 million in missing urban redevelopment funds that made the Monday cover. Betters had done the editing. There were no major red flags. None that she could see, anyway.

Stone's story implicated a low-level city accountant named Peter Turnbill in an embezzlement scheme, with Turnbill shockingly offering a full confession. He admitted that he had "loaned himself" the funds to help pay for his dying mother's care.

"I intend to pay every cent back," he insisted. "I did it, but I'm not a thief."

The "I did it" part of the quote, of course, became the 60-point headline. A picture of Turnbill looking guilty and pale was the front page art, plastered across four columns.

Spurred by the story, the mayor immediately placed Turnbill on administrative leave, vowing a "full and complete investigation into these shocking allegations."

The District Attorney's office quickly obtained a warrant that allowed officers to search the accountant's home and seize his computer and phone. Turnbill answered the door in his pajamas, holding his 18-month son. He looked stunned, his mouth agape, eyes wide. That picture also ran in the paper.

What seemed like another Stone triumph, however, began to slowly unravel.

Competing reporters couldn't confirm much of the story, but that was often true with Stone's exclusives. *How can you confirm facts you can't even get?* A few weeks later, prosecutors quietly backed off, issuing no public statement but confirming that they lacked the evidence to support charges. They had no case.

Turnbill, incensed, demanded a full retraction, alleging that all of the quotes attributed to him were false. Burgess, who took the call from the accountant's lawyer, refused to comply, laughing it off afterward as frivolous. The paper was used to getting sued by people upset with what was written about them, either posturing to influence public opinion or hoping to squeeze out a quick cash settlement.

Burgess soon realized that this case was different. Very different.

In his 35 years in journalism, he'd never seen anything like it. The more he learned, the bigger the lump in his throat became: The family-owned paper, which had been bleeding circulation for years, was suddenly facing a serious risk of a multimillion-dollar verdict.

Adding to the collective anxiety, Stone, always so careful to preserve his notes, written or recorded, couldn't find them. He'd torn apart his apartment and searched every inch of his car and office desk. Betters, aghast, also looked. Together, they found boxes filled with Stone's notebooks that covered his entire six years at the Chronicle, but nothing containing the interview with Turnbill.

Had Stone accidentally thrown them in the trash? Did it happen during one of his benders?

When Betters informed her boss of the unexpected turn of events, Burgess pounded his desk.

"Are you freakin' kidding me!" he bellowed.

Without notes or a recording to support his testimony, a journalist accused of libel was in deep trouble. Especially one with a history of alcohol abuse that wouldn't be difficult to discover. Ask any bartender in town.

The suit seeking $25 million in damages was filed exactly one year after the story was published. As expected, Turnbill accused Stone of making up each of the six damning quotes "out of whole cloth" in order to create a false, sensational narrative designed to sell papers.

There *was* missing money, millions of it – Stone had that part right. But the thief wasn't Turnbill, a mild-mannered, church-going numbers geek. It was Jesse Bakersfield, the man occupying the desk across from Turnbill.

Bakersfield, an auditor, had hacked into his colleague's computer to access the money and cover his tracks, investigators would later discover. When confronted, Bakersfield quickly confessed, claiming he did it to pay for his ailing mother's care, although it turned out that most of the loot funded a lavish lifestyle that included hot women, hotter cars and junkets to the hottest beaches.

Stone had interviewed both men for the story, but somehow, likely in a drunken haze, he attributed Bakersfield's quotes to Turnbill. There was no way for Betters to know that, so she dutifully moved the 2,000-word story along.

After the paper conducted its own review, Burgess wrote a long and embarrassing correction that ran in a box on the front page. The admission apologized to Turnbill and the paper's readers, but did not mention the reporter or his status. The Chronicle wound up settling out of court for an undisclosed amount, rumored to be in the low millions.

A subscription price hike and a round of layoffs soon followed, pushing Stone to the edge of his emotional cliff. His drinking, which was already excessive, intensified to the point that Betters became convinced that his life was at risk.

There was alcohol on his breath and two empty whiskey bottles on the floor when she pulled him out of bed for the last time.

An hour later, she stood with him on the stoop of a detox center she found online. It was called A HAND UP.

There was a number on the steel door but no sign on the building, a former fruit distribution warehouse in a sketchy part of town. Outside, paint was peeling on the walls. Rats scurried down an alley lined with overflowing dumpsters. Betters saw a discarded syringe by her feet.

Did it represent a final high or a sign of surrender?

They stepped inside and her eyebrows jumped. Everything seemed polished and clean. Like a dentist's office. The lobby featured a pair of newish vegan leather couches flanking a metal-and-glass coffee table topped with a large vase filled with fresh flowers – a pleasant assortment of calla lilies, hydrangeas and grasses. Soft jazz flowed from speakers embedded in the ceiling.

Stone was shaking, his dark brown hair matted with sweat. The reverend in charge of the facility appeared before Betters could reach the front desk. He seemed to know they were coming, even though they were there on a strictly walk-in basis.

He greeted each of them warmly, squeezing their hands with both of his. His smile was toothy yet sincere. His eyes sparkled under the fluorescent lights.

"We're here for alcohol treatment," Betters said. "I understand you have beds available, and you're licensed by the state."

"That's correct," Charles Caprice said. "Our programs are being duplicated across the country. We have an extremely high success rate."

"Good to hear," she said, glancing at her watch. "Can I leave him with you and finish filling out the paperwork later?"

"Absolutely. We'll take good care of Mr. Stone. He'll be a new man soon."

"I hope so," she said.

Outside, beside her car, it struck her.

She hadn't mentioned Stone's name.

CHAPTER

FOUR

TURNER ISLAND had no police station, nor a single officer to patrol its freshly swept streets. Cops from the city rarely made the 15-minute drive.

Why should they? Crime on the sleepy, utopian island was virtually non-existent. Plus, the billionaires had their own security details, aided by surveillance cameras and motion sensors inside and out.

Some of the mansions also were equipped with hidden safe rooms, designed to protect both valuables and people in the event of a home-invasion robbery or apocalyptic event. Nobody had ever heard of the comfortable fortified spaces being pressed into service, though.

No, crime wasn't a problem, although the history of the island was steeped in blood.

The mostly flat, Douglas fir-fringed land was originally settled centuries ago by the peaceful Katabe Tribe, which built a small trading post, accessible only by boat, where smoked fish, jerky, animal skins and intricate wood carvings could be purchased.

When tribal elders refused to sell the property to prosperous White settlers in the mid-1800s, the entire indigenous village was burned to the ground. Men, women and children were slaughtered in the most brutal ways imaginable. Few survived to tell the woeful tale, which became known as the Katabe Massacre.

A century later, a modest obelisk memorializing the tragedy was placed on the site of the trading post on the south shore. It was removed during the building of what is now referred to as Billionaire's Row, a boulevard flanked by mature maples and sprawling mansions. The marker's present whereabouts were unknown, much to the chagrin of the city's historical society.

The land became known as Turner Island after William Fields Turner, a respected sea captain and explorer who had served in the Union Navy during the Civil War, became the first White man to build a home there. Many would follow, with each subsequent generation erecting bigger and bigger manors until they became a string of palaces.

Turner Island had always been an oasis seemingly immune to the malaise affecting the outside world. The two biggest concerns of late involved the search for a new headmaster at the private school and upkeep of the only public park – specifically, the health of the cherry trees lining the children's play area.

The headmaster, impressively credentialed, would be paid $250,000 annually, but the governing board at the elite Turner Academy was displeased with the caliber of the candidates thus far and had requested another round – this time advertising the position internationally.

As for the trees that shockingly refused to blossom, replacements were planned thanks to a donation from the Preston Weathers Foundation.

The Weathers family, which made its fortune in oil and lumber, was among the first to homestead on the island and still owned the land on which a ritzy, five-block shopping district called The Commons was built.

It was an odd choice for a name, given the fact that common folks couldn't afford anything for sale there and browsing for browsing's sake was discouraged. Cash wasn't accepted. Metallic credit cards with million-dollar limits were. The most luxurious fashion boutiques were open on an exclusive reservation basis, with repeat customers in dark sunglasses greeted by sunshiny concierges, who'd committed sizes and preferred styles, fabrics and colors to memory.

The district was overseen by a five-member board of directors led by Cicely Weathers, descendant of Preston and proud owner of Tranquility Cove, a spa featuring a variety of massage options, a steam room, facials and weekly yoga and mindful meditation classes. Her pricey Airbnb – the only rental accommodation on the island – filled the space above the spa.

Unlike other communities, there was no ongoing debate about providing sufficient workforce housing. None existed on the island and there were no plans to create any. Baristas, sales people, florists, wine merchants and non-resident household staff shuttled in by car, bus or bicycle. They weren't allowed to arrive before 8 a.m. or leave later than 11 p.m., under regulations imposed by the directorship. On weekends, the hours were limited to noon to 8.

The curfew, punishable by stiff fines, was designed to control noise and traffic, and by all accounts it's been successful. The island was a peaceful place, the quiet disturbed only by gas-powered mowers, squawking seagulls and the occasional gleaming sports car and private helicopter.

Langston shook his head sourly. He hated everything about the island.

Its staggering wealth. Its smug superiority. Its dome-like tranquility.

He turned the van onto Songbrook Lane, aka Billionaire's Row, and cruised past the imposing mansions, many of them snow-white Georgian reproductions with soaring, stately columns in front. The grounds were manicured, with freshly clipped hedges and golf course lawns. Art installations of various sizes and shapes soared, reaching toward the sky. Even the security gates were often draped in ivy and flowering vines, blending seamlessly into the landscaping.

When Langston reached the biggest mansion of them all, he pulled over. He'd previously sketched the exterior, noting the height of the wrought iron fence partially concealed in a towering hedge and the location of the security shack that controlled the gate. Now he wanted to take a closer look.

He got out and walked straight to the shack. A guard in a crisp blue uniform emerged after a few seconds.

"How may I help you?"

"Just wondering if any jobs are available in security," Langston said, peering around the man to see the closed-circuit monitors inside the shack.

"No, but I can give you an application."

"Sure, thanks."

The guard disappeared and Langston noticed that he carried no weapon, not even a taser or pepper spray. He looked down the cobblestone driveway, saw the separate six-car garage. A worker was polishing the limited edition Bugattis and Ferraris. They glinted in the sun like precious jewels, which of course they were.

Langston accepted the application from Sterling Enterprises, offering a pretend smile that looked peculiar on his granite face.

"Good luck," the guard said politely.

Back in the van, Langston sneered. He crushed the paper into a tight ball and tossed it onto the floorboard.

He'd been roaming the island's exclusive south shore for a few hours, pulling over frequently and taking copious notes, but it was time to head back. Father was waiting.

He cruised through The Commons, entered the traffic-slowing roundabout at the end of the bridge. A sunflower-yellow Lamborghini that had been tailgating him blared its horn. The driver, an older man in sunglasses, cursed and wagged a middle finger.

Reflexively, Langston reached for the gun that was always at his side, a semiautomatic Glock, similar to the one he wore as a cop. He gripped the handle, but told himself to be cool. Let the fool pass.

With another honk, the sleek car zoomed around and Langston released his grip.

If it was up to him, he'd raze the sinful island. *Give it back to the Indians.*

But it wasn't up to him. He had his orders to follow and follow them he would. He was what Father would call a "true believer," a born-again Christian who had renounced material pleasures and possessions. He lived a monk-like existence in the rear of the church, where he turned a former storage room into a spartan bedroom.

Inside was only a cheap framed Jesus print, a second-hand table and chair, a cot for a bed, and a forest green steamer trunk doubling as a dresser.

People meeting him for the first time may have thought the stocky, quiet man was introspective, possibly even serene. They couldn't have been more wrong. From a young age, Langston had been a boiling pot of rage. That never changed. Only the rough edges were removed, sanded down by People's Oasis and a charismatic preacher.

It was a well-guarded secret that Langston was once a detective with a cocaine-fueled gambling habit who enjoyed beating people, innocent or not, with his powerful hands. It was one of those savage beatings, involving a 16-year-old Puerto Rican boy turned drug-running snitch, that finally brought him down.

Langston was working homicide in the Bronx at the time, investigating an influx of deadly fentanyl. Record numbers of addicts were dying in the borough, making the case a top priority. The young informant was cultivated as a crucial witness who could expose key players in the operation, but at the last minute he refused to wear a wire as planned. He feared for his mother and younger brother, as well as himself.

"I can't. Too dangerous," he told the cop. "*Muy peligroso.*"

Langston, taken aback, saw months of hard work spiraling down the drain.

"*Dangerous?* You want to see dangerous?" he said, his face suddenly red with fury. Then he hauled off and crushed the boy's nose with his fist.

He didn't stop there. He kept punching until the boy's face was unrecognizable. The wall and floor were splattered with blood.

The boy survived – barely. His mother, who knew about her son's undercover work, filed a complaint. Internal Affairs, which had already been probing Langston for allegedly shaking down immigrant Latinos in order to support his race track wagering and cocaine dependency, closed in fast.

Ultimately a deal was struck. Criminal charges wouldn't be filed if Langston agreed to surrender his badge and never work as a cop again.

Banished from the department, excoriated by the press, he got in his car and drove for days in self-imposed exile. Seemingly wherever the wind blew him. Stoned out of his mind, he ended up on the doorstep of a converted warehouse in a seedy part of a town, far, far away.

A slender, bearded priest with a pleasant smile took him in.

"You'll find peace here," Father said. "And a new life, if you'll have it."

———

The church wasn't much to look at.

Falling well short of the biblical goal of being "a manifestation of heaven on Earth," People's Oasis was housed in a former oil-soaked tool factory.

For 20 years, the blockish building sat vacant in the tenderloin across from unused railroad tracks, becoming a home to vagrants and a nesting ground for pigeons, who flew in and out through the broken windows. The exterior metal siding was rusting. The flat roof was leaking. The old roll-up doors by the loading dock had stopped working long ago.

The building was in such poor condition, even the real estate company trying to sell it called it a "fixer-upper" in need of new owners "not afraid to roll up your sleeves and rise to the challenge."

Nobody rose to the challenge, even at a bargain price. That is, until Charles Caprice came along one drizzly afternoon. At the time, he was a little-known street preacher whose ministry was helping the homeless.

Touring the structure, he took note of the solid beams and thick concrete floors. He looked at the failing windows and imagined stained glass. At the end of the main room, he envisioned a pulpit. Behind that, a large, simple cross. And in the middle, as many pews as would fit. Enough to seat hundreds.

"I'll take it," he told the real estate agent. "It's wonderful."

"Wonderful for *what?*" she asked.

"A church."

She nearly spit out her caramel latte.

"You're going to turn this … this decrepit industrial building, into a *church?*" She spun around theatrically, making a sour face. "There are other properties I can show you that are much more appropriate."

"My dear lady," Caprice said warmly, "the Lord has brought me here. I do not know His plan, but I understand now what I must do."

"And what's that?"

"Take my ministry to a higher level, so I may serve Him better."

"Reverend, with all due respect, I don't think you know what you're getting into here. The cost of the repairs alone will be considerable. And then to make this a church …"

The priest merely smiled and patted her shoulder.

"Whatever it takes," he said. "Please understand: I have little choice in the matter. I'll be at your office tomorrow to sign the papers."

The next day, People's Oasis Church was born. Father did some of the minor repairs himself, but most of the jobs were tackled by enthusiastic volunteers, including a few contractors and carpenters, eager to repay the pastor for past acts of kindness.

Beautiful stained-glass windows depicting the Garden of Eden, Noah's Ark and The Last Supper arrived one day, a gift from an artist whose grown son had wound up on the streets after getting laid off. Caprice gave him a job and a safe place to live until he could regain his footing.

Within two months, from a donated pulpit made by hand out of oak, the first sermon was delivered. Two dozen people on folding chairs listened intently. Wooden pews made by a talented craftsman who'd joined the flock were installed a few months later. Soon, the church could seat 200 worshippers comfortably.

Sunday attendance had swelled to 400 when People's Oasis opened its first homeless shelter, taking over a vacant building next door. When that proved successful, city officials came to call.

Would the church be interested in expanding its operation, reaching other hard-hit neighborhoods?

Caprice told them he'd pray on it.

Two weeks later, he accepted his first grant, totaling $905,000, with few strings attached. City Hall was eager to look like it was addressing a thorny issue in a humane way.

When the second shelter opened, a picture of the priest and Mayor Salvatore Pucci shaking hands outside the remodeled two-story building ran inside the Metro section of the Chronicle. It was the first of many news items to come, as the church's reach rapidly expanded and the grants doubled, tripled and then quadrupled.

Caprice never sought media attention, but when it came he was always accommodating.

TV news crews often followed him as he walked the bleak streets around the church, stopping to console the men and women camping outside with cardboard for blankets. Most had a sad story to tell about their freefalls; how they'd come to rely on soup kitchens and handouts, belongings tucked in a tattered backpack or shopping cart.

Caprice knew many of them by their first names. He'd gently offer them help, but never prod or push. It was their decision to make. He'd simply give them options and let them mull it over.

"Joseph, nice to see you," he said, greeting a man sitting cross-legged on the sidewalk. He was a stone-faced veteran with PTSD who'd been in and out of the church and its social welfare programs.

"That's a nice jacket you've got."

It was a crisp fall afternoon, in the low 40s, and the coat looked lightly used and warm – lined denim with a wool hood that Joseph was using to block the wind. There was an American flag patch on the right shoulder.

"Someone dropped it off when I was sleeping. Was it you?"

As the cameras rolled, Caprice laughed. "No, Joseph. Looks like you have another guardian angel."

"Yeah, mebbe."

Caprice noticed the old coffee can Joseph was using to collect handouts, HELP A VETERAN scrawled across the front. The can was empty. Not even a quarter.

"It's turning cold, my friend. Would you like a bunk in the shelter? Hot shower and some food?"

Joseph scratched his whiskered chin. "Heard it was all full up."

"We always make room for our friends. Tell them I said so."

"Okay, thanks. Mebbe I will."

"Good. And come to services tomorrow if you can. I'll be sharing an important message."

"Oh padre, you know I ain't much for Bible talk."

"That's fine. You decide. It'll be warm inside. We got the old furnace fixed."

Caprice bent down and whispered something in the man's ear, some kind of prayer. The veteran's eyes watered, but he said nothing.

"I've known Joseph for several years," Caprice told the TV reporter as they continued down the block in search of souls to salve. "He's a good man. Just down on his luck, like so many others."

"Will he use the shelter tonight?" the reporter asked.

"Probably not. He's very proud. But the important thing, the message

I tried to deliver, is that he knows he won't ever be turned away if he needs help."

"Why do you think your homeless programs have been so successful compared to others?"

Caprice stopped and thought for a few seconds.

"We're faith-based. We never use force like the police, dragging them off to jail or to rehab. So, the people we serve trust us more. When you've faced all the adversity these people have, trust is so vital. I think that's the biggest difference."

"You have contracts with the city that now top $8 million a year. Why should taxpayers trust *you* with all that money?"

"Ooh, such a tough question," Caprice said, clutching his chest for effect. Then he grew serious. "I guess the answer lies in the results. By combining treatment and counseling with housing, we've transitioned more than 3,500 people off the streets. A majority are back in the work force, contributing to the local economy. If every city in America achieved *that*, homelessness would no longer be the existential crisis that it is today."

"All this work, with so many lives in the balance, it seems awfully stressful," the reporter said. "How do you cope?"

"I meditate every day, take walks in the woods when I can. Since I was a boy, I've always found peace under the waves. There's nothing like being inside nature's aquarium to slow things down, put it all in perspective. Wherever I go, I bring my scuba gear."

"Nice. Final question, pastor: Are you thinking about getting into politics, possibly running for mayor? Your congregation continues to grow and your sermons have been creating quite a stir. The videos have gone viral."

That was true. Caprice had been turning up the volume of late, chastising the One Percenters for "worshipping the almighty dollar" and turning a blind eye to suffering in the world. After watching one of the videos, a U.S. senator flew across the country to have lunch with the pastor, commending him for his tireless work on the issue.

After that, People's Oasis became a favorite of the progressives. Caprice attended some of their events and luncheons, prompting a surge in donations, even though he never asked for a cent. The influx of money allowed the organization to hire more staff, add beds and improve services and outreach.

The church itself remained austere, with none of the familiar ornate trappings. The simple cross on the wall wasn't swapped out for a gilded one. The utilitarian pulpit remained. The concrete floors stayed bare.

Even the pastor's quarters were small and sparsely furnished – the only luxury being the stacks of books and pamphlets that seemed to sprout everywhere. The topics were wide-ranging, from treatises by ancient theologians to modern dissertations on the human condition. And, for good measure, an Orwellian novel or two.

By all accounts, Caprice was coming into his own. To many, he was a folk hero, crusading on behalf of the have-nots. To cynics, he was too good to be true. Nobody could be that selfless, they thought.

As for the notion of entering the political arena, Caprice laughed.

"There's no time for such nonsense," he told the reporter.

———

Scowling, the mayor sat behind his gleaming cherrywood desk, stubby fingers braided behind his head.

The preacher was on his mind. He was constantly on Pucci's mind of late.

"I was there last week for the sermon, Upps. He had the crowd eating out of his hands. It was remarkable. Utterly remarkable. He's like MLK reborn, for God's sake."

Born in Egypt and educated in England, Omar Upps had become one of America's brightest political strategists. Over the past decade, none of his candidates had lost an election, an impressive record that rocketed his fees into the stratosphere.

He harbored doubts about this race, however. The latest polls showed Pucci, the two-term incumbent, losing narrowly to Caprice – and the crusading reverend wasn't even on the ballot. Not yet.

Upps rubbed his shiny bald head. He adjusted his round, wire-rimmed glasses. On his lap was a four-inch stack of papers, including the latest polling numbers and focus group summaries.

"Sal, I watched the livestream," he said. "He's got charisma, that's true. And every day, his flock grows. That makes him powerful."

"If he enters the race, I'm toast."

"Not *toast*. You have important allies, big-money contributors you can tap at will and a solid get-out-the-vote network, but it'd be awfully close. That grassroots support he's garnered is impressive."

"What are we going to do about it?"

Seemingly deep in thought, the strategist rose to his feet and stepped to the third-floor window, causing a pigeon on the ledge to take flight.

"Watch him closely, do some digging," he said after a few moments. "Find his weaknesses. Exploit them if necessary."

"If he *has* any weaknesses. His followers think he walks on water. It's my own damn fault, too. I created this monster by pulling the strings that gave him those contracts."

"True, but you also got a rather large monkey off your back. The homeless issue was eating into your support. Ditto on the drug front. Your favorables went up after Caprice took over."

The mayor thumped the alarming report Upps had placed on the desk. "Yeah, but Caprice's numbers are off the charts. The public loves the sonofabitch."

"Of course, none of this matters if he doesn't run," the adviser replied. His brown eyes were magnified by the thick lenses, making him seem more intense. "He's on record denying any interest in politics. It sounds convincing."

"Bullshit. Everybody craves power and influence – even him. Maybe especially him. For his pet projects, if nothing else. I'll ask you again: What's our plan?"

"For now, we wait," Upps said. "The candidate filing deadline is two weeks away."

"Shouldn't we start doing our opposition research now? Get a head start?"

The consultant shook his head.

"We'll know what he's up to soon enough," he said.

CHAPTER
FIVE

THE GUESTS WERE due to arrive any minute, and there were so many things to do. So many things.

Cicely Weathers bounced from room to room, armed with an upright vacuum and orange microfiber towels, vanquishing dust as she went. When she got to the living room, she moved the arrangement of freshly cut daylilies for the third time, then shuffled and fluffed the velvet throw pillows on the sofa.

Weathers took pride in her Superhost status and glowing five-star reviews – so much so that she couldn't trust all the cleaning to a maid. She did the final buffing herself, down to the handwritten, personalized greeting on the slender chalkboard hanging by the door: WELCOME BRIDGET AND BARRY! Beneath the names were two ornate hearts, also hand-drawn.

"There, that's better!" she declared out loud, only to suddenly remember to check the crumb tray on the toaster.

Forty-something and fit, Weathers was attractive, with hazel eyes and a sunny smile. She was also wealthy – heir to a considerable fortune. She lived at the east end of Billionaire's Row in a stretched

Colonial with her bank executive husband Darren Andrews, a wirehaired pointer named Arrow and a lethargic gray-and-white rabbit dubbed Fat Sam.

A comfortable life, without question. Even after Darren's fling at the banking conference in Indianapolis and, later, following months of couples counseling and trust-building exercises, the uneasy realignment of their marriage.

Still, when the neighbors flaunted their yachts, imported marble fountains and statuary, plastic surgery and movie-star lifestyles, she cringed. Such displays seemed distasteful, even crude. She'd always painted herself in primary colors: as a wife, a small business owner, a daughter.

While her husband drove a Jaguar coupe, her vehicle was a practical silver Volvo SUV, now six years old. Well-appointed, but not particularly luxurious. She picked it because it was built to last, big enough to haul stuff and boasted one of the industry's best crash-test safety ratings.

The Airbnb also reflected her personality: classy and comfortable; not ostentatious. To cover the walls of her rental, she could have raided her parents' rare art collection that had been handed down and was now gathering dust in a basement. She went with simple landscapes instead, painted by local artists.

Weathers eyed the sparkling kitchen one last time, looking for anything out of place. Any object that required last-minute polishing.

"Done!"

She was putting the vacuum away when she heard the turbocharged growl of a car pulling into the lot behind the building. Weathers primped her honey blonde hair in the mirror and was at the door when the bell rang.

Bridget and Barry Bortles, in from Atlanta, were making their sixth visit. Rather than stay on the mainland, they preferred the quiet of the island, and Weathers' Airbnb was the only option. Hotels of any size were strictly forbidden.

Weathers gave them each an obligatory hug. They were husband-and-wife executives at a top-tier PR firm that specialized in damage control for sports figures, movie stars and politicians who'd been publicly accused of bad things.

Several of their clients lived on the island, including a basketball player turned rapper who called himself Shock Jock. He was facing a dozen counts of sexual assault involving three underage girls. His record label was getting ready to drop him.

"We're happy to be back," Bridget said with the whitest of smiles. "It's so peaceful here."

"Yeah, no screams and police sirens," put in Barry as he hauled suitcases to the bedroom. "You wouldn't believe what our downtown has become. Bums everywhere. Parks full of tents. Urine on the pickleball courts. *Pickleball!*"

"Disgusting," Bridget added, wrinkling her button nose.

"I hope you have a pleasant stay," Weathers said, knowing that the couple would spend the bulk of their time with ignominious clients facing jail time. In her mind, those residents were the few bad apples marring a beautiful tree. She secretly wished they would leave.

"If there's anything either of you need, don't hesitate to reach out."

"Thank you, Cicely," Barry said, inspecting his Brioni suit for wrinkles. "You're the best."

———

The fact that Weathers felt compelled to attend one of Caprice's sermons befuddled her husband.

"He despises people like us – the so-called ultra-rich," he told her. "Why are you so interested?"

"I don't know. He's just so … *passionate* about the issue, I suppose. And a lot of what he says is true, Darren. We do need to care more. We need to give more."

He groaned but said nothing, not wanting to trigger another fight. His wife's sudden obsession seemed to come out of nowhere, but then again, he often tuned out the non-essentials.

"Okay, but you can watch the sermons on your laptop. They stream them live. I don't feel comfortable with you being in that neighborhood. It's not safe."

"It's Sunday morning," she said, rolling her eyes. "I hardly think I'll be mugged going to church. And I have been watching the services. They're quite something. I want to experience it in person. The energy, the emotion …"

"He's not Mick Jagger. Or the second coming of Jesus, for that matter."

"I don't expect you to understand."

"At least take Joey. Have him walk you to the door."

Joey Fallone managed their estate and oversaw security, checking the alarms and reviewing the camera footage. He was on the grounds every day, controlling the comings and goings of the part-time cook, gardening crew and other workers, but also walking the perimeter with squinty eyes, as if a criminal could spring from the 7-foot-high English laurel hedges at any instant.

There had never been a problem. No break-ins, no burglaries. Just a brash squirrel that chewed through some electrical wires one day and got electrocuted. Still, you never knew, so Fallone kept walking.

Weathers sighed. "I'll take Joey if it'll make you feel better. Sure you don't want to go with me?"

"I'm sure. That kind of stuff isn't my cup of tea. Besides, the game is on."

A short time later, she found Fallone on the back lawn. The 41-year-old bachelor was shirtless, doing his usual morning taekwondo. He resembled a young Keanu Reeves, with his short-cropped inky hair and sculpted physique.

Weathers paused to watch him do his graceful spins, punching the air and kicking in a rhythmic way.

She found it raw and sensual, unlike her yoga and meditation classes which were more about cultivating a mind-body harmony. She would sometimes find herself looking down from her bedroom window, seeing the sweat glistening on his chest as her own pulse quickened.

When he saw her, he stopped and grabbed a towel.

"Joey, sorry to disturb your exercise," she said. "I'm in need of an escort."

She explained the situation, and he whole-heartedly agreed with the safety concerns.

"It's a rough area," the former beat cop said, hurriedly buttoning his cotton shirt. "Lots of stabbings, fights between homeless people, that sort of stuff. It's good that I'll be taking you. You need me to sit in church?"

"Only if you want to. I'm fine by myself."

"Well, if it's alright with you, I'll stay in the car. There's a couple of podcasts I'd like to check out."

She checked her watch. "We should go. How long of a drive is it?"

"Oh, not long. About 25 minutes this time of day."

"Great. Mind driving the Volvo while I return a few messages?"

"No problem, ma'am."

"*Ma'am?* Really? You're making me feel old. I've told you a dozen times to call me Cicely."

"Sorry, ma'am. *Cicely*, I mean. Geez, this may take a while to get used to."

She smiled, lighting up her face. He melted a bit, struck by her beauty. He always did. But those thoughts, about a married woman who was his boss, made him uncomfortable. He quickly tried flushing them out of his head.

"Can I ask you a question?"

"Of course."

"Why do you want to go? To that church, I mean."

Why did everyone find her interest in People's Oasis so strange, she wondered. It's not like she was the type to get bamboozled by some smooth-talking charlatan. She came across a clip of the priest on social media and got intrigued. Simple as that.

"There's something about the preacher," she answered after a moment. "His message resonates with me, in a strange way. Maybe it's guilt, maybe not. I think the only way to really process my feelings is to see this man in the flesh."

"Yeah, I grew up poor. My parents struggled," Fallone said. "I get it – how his message hits home for a lot of folks."

A few minutes later, the SUV left the circular driveway, pausing for the security gate to slowly yawn open.

Soon, the Volvo was sweeping over the choppy blue water toward the city, its gray skyscrapers looming on the horizon.

"I met him once," Fallone said in a low voice.

"Oh really?"

"Yeah, a few years ago. I was clearing out some homeless people and he suddenly appeared, like out of nowhere. He told me to release them. In a nice way, I mean. Very polite. Smiling even."

The driver glanced at the rear-view mirror, saw she was paying close attention.

"You'll probably think this is funny, but there was something about his eyes," he told his passenger. "A kind of glow. Something almost … magical. Sort of hard to explain."

"What about the homeless people? Did you let them stay?"

"Sure did. Why mess with God?"

CHAPTER

SIX

WHEN WEATHERS arrived, the place was packed.

She managed to squeeze in toward the back, taking a seat at the end of a long pew. Looking around, she saw an interesting mix of people, from those with greasy hair and third-hand clothes to socialites and celebrities checking out the latest sensation.

There was a hum of anticipation in the crowd, something that couldn't be captured on the church videos focused almost entirely on the pulpit.

A burly man suddenly appeared in the aisle, glaring at someone in the seat across from Weathers.

"Hand it over," he whispered in a harsh tone. The woman reluctantly obliged, pulling a half-drunk pint bottle out of her coat. "You know the rules."

"I want it back after," she hissed.

The man disappeared with the hooch. Weathers took him to be Langston, the man who Caprice, like a late-night TV host, had elevated to sidekick status minus the punchlines.

Weathers scanned the sanctuary again, noticing the overflow balcony in the back that had recently been added. There must be more than 800 people, she marveled.

"This should be good," the unshaved man next to her said in giddy anticipation. His body odor made her eyes sting, but she managed a polite nod.

A hush fell over the crowd and then there he was. The star of the show.

Caprice entered with a practiced stage performer's swagger, swathed in his vestment, priestly robes flowing behind him. His thick hair bounced off his shoulders. He was slender and taller than she'd expected.

The pastor stepped up to the pulpit and smiled broadly, radiating warmth. With him, he had nothing. Not even a Bible.

"Welcome, my friends," he began, raising his hands. "Praise the Lord."

"Praise the Lord!" the crowd thundered.

Caprice uttered the Lord's Prayer in a silky cadence that gave Weathers goosebumps. Many in the audience joined in.

He made the signs of the cross then recited another prayer that floated across the pews like a comforting cloud.

Three young Black women in white robes ascended the stairs and gathered in front of the mic as the pastor stepped aside. Joined by a man playing guitar, they began to sing, in a high-pitched angelic way.

Worshippers joined in, many rising to their feet.

Weathers, raised by tolerant Methodists, had been to plenty of religious services – some of which had bored her to tears. But this was different: Soulful Gospel meets evangelical Christian. Stirred, she found herself tapping her foot. The man next to her was enraptured, rocking back and forth.

Caprice himself was grooving, dancing in place, eyes angled skyward.

When the singing was over, the priest asked everyone to introduce themselves to their neighbors in the pews. An offering basket made the rounds. Then Caprice settled in for his sermon.

"I see the mayor is here," he said, drawing a mix of applause and jeers. "Thank you for coming."

"Also, I see Mr. Hugo Sterling. Your presence here today is heartening."

Sterling was the founder and CEO of the company that built rocket ships for NASA and gave rides into near space to anyone willing to pay the fare, currently set at $25 million a flight.

He belonged to the world's most elite club as one of a handful of centibillionaires – those whose fortunes top $100 billion. He made his wealth in biotech, including a breakthrough drug called Evermore that slowed the aging process when injected once a month. Despite its high cost, at $44,449 a shot, the drug proved so popular that workers in his North American factories attempted to unionize. Sterling responded by shuttering the factories and opening new ones in Vietnam and Thailand.

Weathers had a number of run-ins with him over gaudy additions to his Turner Island estate, including a 5,000-square-foot guest house with a solarium. Some of the problems he caused himself. His newest superyacht, with its built-in helipad and swimming pools, was so massive it couldn't be moored off his dock.

What's he doing here, she wondered. *Probably curious like me.*

"We have another special guest today, one who I am particularly excited about," the pastor continued. "Joseph Blanchard Jr., welcome."

A man in a hooded jacket shrunk deeper into his seat.

"Please forgive Joseph for being a little shy. Going to church isn't his 'jam,' as he puts it." That line drew a few chuckles. "But folks like him are the reason this church exists. We support him, not the other way around, and that's the way it should be, isn't it?

"You see, Joseph served our country with honor and distinction. Five years ago, he was overseas, protecting one of our embassies from a terrorist attack. Seriously wounded by a rocket blast, he was sent home to recover.

"He learned to walk again, but he nearly lost everything just the same. Like millions of other Americans, in the richest land the world has ever known, Joseph ended up on the streets. His PTSD made it impossible to keep a job, and the meager assistance he received every month wasn't enough to live on. Not nearly enough.

"So, Joseph found himself camping, often right outside here, on these dreary sidewalks. And there, like countless others, he succumbed to the illicit drugs infesting our city. Even worse, he experienced another plague – the lack of compassion society has for the downtrodden and homeless. They'd step over him as he slept, needle in his arm. They'd steal the few dollars in his rusted can. They'd mock him.

"And, so I ask all of you: What would Jesus do? Would He consider Joseph a lost cause? Would He give up hope?"

"NO!" the crowd shouted in unison.

"Of course not. Jesus preached love and compassion. He would wash the feet of his disciples. So, why is it so hard for us today to follow the Lord's example? Why are the wealthiest among us not doing more to spare people such anguish, such obvious pain? Why can't we give them a helping hand? Why do we ignore their hardship?"

Sterling squirmed in his seat.

"As I said, we live in the wealthiest country in the history of the world," Caprice continued. "But most of that wealth is going to the top 1 percent – more money than they would ever know what to do with. Billions upon billions.

"At the same time, millions of people in America are struggling. They have no savings or insurance. Often, they lack the money needed to see a doctor when they're sick. Every day, they worry if their aging car breaks down that they'll lose their jobs. And if they lose their jobs, they can't feed their families. They live on the edge of ruin. So very close to the edge.

"And still the richest people in this country – in this world – turn a blind eye. They are too busy worshipping the accumulation of great wealth to be moved, or to even notice at all. They turn from the teachings of God, from their fellow man, from love and compassion, to kneel day and night before their golden idol, thinking only of money and profit.

"I ask you, my friends, what is the morality of this? Is it moral when the top 1 percent has as much wealth as the bottom 90 percent? Is it moral when they don't give a damn about anyone less fortunate than themselves?"

"NO!" the congregants shouted.

Caprice nodded.

"I agree. My message for you all today is to search your collective soul. Ask yourselves: Am I doing enough? Personally, I know that I am not. I know that as a certainty because the job isn't done. This church – the shelters, the programs, it's all just a start. An encouraging start, yes, but let's not fool ourselves. It's really the first step in a long journey. So, let us praise Jesus and ask Him to give us the strength to continue on our path – the path of righteousness and resistance. Amen."

"AMEN!"

The choir returned for a couple more rousing gospel songs, this time backed up by a drummer as well. Then Caprice recited a closing prayer and bid everyone a pleasant day.

He wasn't Jagger, but the service sparked something inside Weathers. Something heartwarming and hopeful.

So, this is how it feels to be under his spell.

———

As he returned to the car, Fallone felt a bit embarrassed at having portrayed the area around the church as a combat zone.

Looking around, he noticed there wasn't a homeless person in sight. No signs of the familiar makeshift encampment. The sidewalks seemed oddly spotless. The usual litter of spent bottles and empty food cartons was gone.

He'd never seen the area so clean. While he hadn't been back since his encounter with Caprice, his friends on the force complained nonstop about the squalid camp and its rampant drug and alcohol abuse – and the church's apparent tolerance of the situation.

Fallone figured the church cleared out the drunks and junkies on Sundays to create a better impression for guests and worshippers, plus a safer path in and out. But moving out the homeless people for appearances' sake didn't jive with Caprice's stated mission. His kindness-first philosophy.

Where did they put them, the security man wondered. He'd seen some down-and-outers entering the church minutes ago, presumably to attend the service, but the encampment typically ballooned to a hundred or more.

Where did they all go?

Fallone shrugged. "Not my concern anymore," he said under his breath.

He was about to get in the Volvo and cue up a podcast on outdoor survival when something caught his eye: a row of trucks neatly parked in the lot next door.

His curiosity kindled, Fallone walked over to take a closer look. He counted eight identical vehicles. White, medium-duty Ford box trucks. There were no markings on the sides, indicating likely rentals.

One of the trucks had its rear roll-up door open, and he peeked inside. It was filled with sandbags, wooden crates, toilet paper and bottled water. And was that scuba gear? *How strange.*

He leaned in to take a closer look, focusing on the crates. He was about to remove the lid from one of them when a giant hand squeezed his.

"This is private property."

Fallone turned and saw a large man with angry eyes and a tree-trunk neck. There was a telltale outline of a pistol against the man's jacket.

"Hey, easy now," Fallone said. "I was just looking."

The man slowly released his hold. His expression softened, but only a little. With his ham fists and broad shoulders, he looked like a bouncer, or worse, a gangster.

Fallone didn't want a piece of that action. He didn't carry a gun anymore. It wouldn't be a fair fight.

"I'll be on my way," he murmured. "Sorry to bother."

A two-way radio clipped to the man's belt suddenly crackled and he pulled it out while maintaining fierce eye contact with Fallone. "I'll be right there," he said.

To the interloper, he snarled, "Take a hike."

After backpedaling a few steps, Fallone returned to the car, moving as fast as he could without running. From a safe distance, he watched with relief as the hulking enforcer disappeared inside the church.

What was that about?

———

After the service, the pastor worked the center aisle, shaking each of the many hands extended toward him. He seemed to pay extra attention to people like Joseph, the unbathed and hungry.

When Caprice reached Weathers, he paused to study her face.

"Welcome, Cicely," he said cordially.

Weathers looked surprised. "How do you know my name? We've never met."

"No, but I know you just the same. From Turner Island." He gave a wink and grinned, enjoying the small suspense he'd created. "I try to keep up on what's going on out there … in a heaven-and-hell sort of way, no offense."

"I see."

"I knew you'd come."

"Why's that?"

"It came to me in a vision."

His luminous eyes held her gaze. She found the effect vaguely hypnotic and forced herself to look down, studying her black pumps.

"Well, I must confess that I rather enjoyed the service," she said sheepishly.

"Nice of you to say. I'll be seeing you again soon, Cicely. We'll talk more then."

Puzzled by the remark, she watched him leave.

Caprice exited the sanctuary in long strides, the resolute Langston by his side. A column of followers strained to keep pace.

With their determined faces and practiced formation, they looked like soldiers, Weathers thought.

CHAPTER

SEVEN

THREE DAYS without a drop. Strangely enough, Stone felt worse, not better.

He had just emptied his well-endowed liquor cabinet, dumping the booze down the kitchen drain. The chore took the better part of an hour, filling two large boxes with empty bottles of various sizes and hues. As he did so, his hands shook. His throat was sandpaper dry.

Stone figured he'd bottomed out when he did his time in detox and was forced to face the bitter reality of his blackout-inducing binge drinking by Reverend Caprice. It was a form of self-mutilation, he discovered. A toxic response to the trauma and turmoil in his life.

He'd sworn he'd never need treatment again. He'd never crawl into the same woeful pit of despair. But, a few short months later, when he screwed up a story and became a liability, he was back on a bar stool drowning himself in hopes of forgetting what couldn't be forgotten.

In the gritty aftermath of that night, the effort it took to find his abandoned car seemed Herculean.

The bruised Subaru had been towed to an impound lot, he discovered. It had been parked on top of the sidewalk at a crazy angle, blocking an alley. He had imagined climbing a steep hill to get to the final bar on his crawl, but the watering hole was really around the corner. Those revelations made him shudder because it wasn't simply a night of heavy drinking. It was a full-fledged, bonafide relapse.

Was that the real reason he agreed to go out to Turner Island? Because maybe he could squeeze another therapy session out of Caprice?

Stone shook his head sadly. He was too effed up to have any answers. On the verge of tears, he stood, staring at the boozy trash for a long time. The trance was interrupted by a call.

"Hey, Sally."

"Sorry to call so late."

Stone only then realized it was nighttime. "No prob. Why are you calling?"

"Just checking on how you're doing."

"Yeah, well, I've dumped every drop down the drain. So, that's something."

"Good for you. How're you doing mentally?"

"Better since that meeting. Hey, I'm going out to Turner Island at 7 in the morning. The priest who heads People's Oasis Church will be there, says he has a big story for me."

"Oh *really*." Betters sounded skeptical. Stone knew that tone all too well. But he was skeptical, too.

"I know, I know. It's probably nothing, but I told him I'd be there."

"That's the dude who runs the detox centers, including the one I took you to, right?"

"The very same. Charles Caprice, the darling of the far left."

"Strange."

"What?"

"There's something weird about him. Like he's up to something with all those followers. It's like a cult."

"Ah, it's probably just a publicity stunt. I'll be in and out. We'll talk after, have a good laugh."

"Isn't Caprice the one who counseled you during rehab?"

"Yeah."

"I see. So, you feel like you owe him one?"

"Not really. I'm just curious."

"Sure thing. … Still sober? Sorry, but I'm supposed to ask. ME's orders."

"Hundred percent." Three days and counting, but the ice was awfully thin.

"Good, now stay out of the bars and we can get back to doing what we're paid for. You know, kick-ass journalism."

"Amen to that."

"Amen? You *are* ready to see a pastor."

They both laughed. Stone hung up and lifted one of the boxes. There was a recycling station in the basement of the Tudor Arms.

He entered the long sterile hall, sandals slapping against the low-cut carpet. The bottles sounded their death rattle.

It made him thirsty.

———

The security man spotted the van driving slowly past the estate and thought little of it – until it made a second pass, just as slow.

Grabbing compact binoculars from the tool bag slung over his shoulder, Fallone saw the driver looking out the windows, seemingly surveying the boulevard.

Fallone zeroed in on the man behind the wheel and his jaw dropped.

It was the muscled enforcer who'd scared him off the church property the other day. There was no mistaking that fearsome mug.

I'll be damned. What are you doing here?

Before the van disappeared for good, Fallone got the plate number, jotting it on his wrist in black ink.

There were a dozen innocent explanations for the van's presence on Billionaire's Row, but it was another slow day in paradise and he had some free time. Besides, he'd been curious about those box trucks and their mysterious contents. It had been bugging him for the last two days.

What was he missing?

Fallone called in the plate, tapping one of his pals in the police department.

"It's probably nothing, Bonnie, but if you could run it, I'd be grateful."

"Sure, Joey. Maybe you can land me one of those cushy island jobs."

"You can take this one when I die of boredom."

A few minutes later, Bonnie called back with the information. The van, she said, was registered locally, to People's Oasis.

Fallone wondered why Caprice would send someone out to Turner Island. It clearly wasn't to scout real estate. The average home price was a staggering $25 million. To build a house, you'd have to demolish the existing one – an even pricier proposition.

Nah, this guy looked like he was casing the neighborhood. Something wasn't right.

He called the station back, this time reaching a detective he knew.

"How ya doin' Mike? This is Joey."

"Joey! *Paisano!* How the hell are you?"

"Couldn't be better. You know, living the dream and all."

"You really scored with that gig of yours. Money for nothing, right?"

"Pretty much. Hey Mike, have you guys been hearing any chatter about People's Oasis? Anything unusual going on?"

"You mean other than that bum lover doing his shtick? Haven't heard a peep. Why?"

"I was at the church for my client a few days ago and the entire tent city was gone. I mean erased. *Poof.* A whole fleet of trucks was parked outside. One of them was filled with sandbags and crates with stenciled markings that looked military. And, a few minutes ago, a van registered to the church was here, cruising Billionaire's Row really slow. The driver was looking around, taking notes."

"You ain't never seen a driver write something down before? Maybe he was doing a survey or something."

"This looked suspicious. I recognized him from the church. He basically ran me off when I started snooping."

The detective snorted. "C'mon, Joey. Nothing bad ever happens out there. Can't remember the last time anyone from here went on a call. Maybe an oldster wanders off. Maybe a curious cat gets stuck in a tree. That's about it."

"Yeah, yeah, I know. But something's off. I got this feeling."

"Hoo boy. Last time you had a feeling, I wound up filling out a ton of paperwork."

"I remember. Quite a bust."

"Look, for old time's sake, maybe I'll head over to the church, check out those trucks of yours."

"I'd appreciate it. Please lemme know if you find anything."

"Will do, pal. And if a job there opens up …"

"You'll be the first to know."

Fallone searched the street below one more time. Nothing. He walked past Ernesto, the pruning shears-wielding gardener, and went back inside the main house, pausing in the wainscotted foyer. Should he inform his clients about his suspicions?

Nope, he decided. Why alarm them unnecessarily? Like Mike said, nothing bad ever happens out here.

Then he remembered the line about the cat and laughed.

CHAPTER

EIGHT

THE HELICOPTER roared over the water, hovered briefly, then came to rest at a sprawling estate.

Hugo Sterling climbed out, ducking under the swooshing blades, and was immediately greeted by members of the in-house security detail, looking polished in their mirrored sunglasses and communication earpieces.

"Welcome back, sir," they said.

Moments later, he was mobbed by his pride and joy: a pair of impeccably groomed Tibetan mastiffs. The giant black dogs leaped at their owner, nearly knocking him to the ground. He named them after stars, in keeping with his obsession with outer space.

"Down Proxima!" he commanded. "Down Antares!"

"They never listen," a woman's voice said. "They may trample you to death in your old age, darling. Out of affection, of course."

Shedding his pets, he ascended the broad stone steps to a lush outdoor terrace. It was dotted with Romanesque statues and featured a huge gilded fountain inspired by the Palace of Versailles. Water spilled from the mouths of porcelain fish into a tiled pool.

Ashley Sterling offered her husband a dry martini with two olives, which she had the butler make the moment the upstairs windows started to tremble and she knew the copter, a luxurious Hill HX50 in emerald green, was returning.

He accepted the drink without saying a word, suddenly annoyed that she wouldn't be joining him.

She was only starting to show, but soon would be trading clingy designer clothes for a maternity wardrobe. Those thoughts threatened to further sour the magnate's mood. The baby was her idea, not his. She thought it'd give him a reason to be home more often, bridge the growing distance between them. But he had a business empire to run. And he knew a trap when he saw one.

"How was the service?" Ashley inquired as she settled into a chaise lounge.

Looking more like a celebrity than the part-time lingerie model she had been, she wore oversized sunglasses and a silk dress that accentuated her curves. Her auburn hair was in a bun, full lips painted ruby red.

The age difference between them had been a constant topic for the gossip mags. He was 64, with a paunch that gave him a slight waddle. She was 31 and gorgeous, with toned dancer's legs.

"Terrible," he said, taking a sip. "He went on and on about the sins of the wealthy. I felt everybody looking at me and judging."

"Poor dear. You can't say I didn't warn you." She rubbed her swollen belly. Noticing, he frowned.

"I had to go. *Once.* We all do," he said, waving at the neighboring mansions. "Make our little pilgrimage to Mecca. Pray at his altar. Pretend to be sympathetic to the cause, whatever it is."

She thought that was funny, but he knitted his brow.

"Our friend the reverend has become a powerful force," he said, lowering his voice to a conspiratorial whisper. "Those followers of his, if he turns them against us … well, we need to stay on his good side, I think. For now."

"For now?"

He took another sip. "Usually a meteoric rise is followed by an equally powerful collapse. That's one of the truths of the universe."

"Spoken like a true spaceman," she teased.

"It's not funny. We're a nation of two classes: the haves and have-nots, and resentment is building. Our preacher is just the man to start some kind of civil war. And if that happens, we're hopelessly outnumbered."

"Darling, let's not talk about that again," she said. "We're nearly packed and I want to think happy thoughts."

"A thousand apologies. Like I said, I had to go one time to see what he was up to." He forced a smile. "Looking forward to Belize. Magnificent this time of year. Amazing sunsets."

"Please, no work this time. You look so stressed."

"I'll do my best, but the launch is in two months. We simply can't have another failure."

She made a pouty face and he relented. "Okay, no calls. Just an email or two."

"Yay!" she declared, brightening. "I'll tell Maria to get everything stocked at the villa. The yacht is docked there, yes? It'll be *wonderful.*"

"Whatever makes you happy."

Sterling said the words but didn't believe them. When he married her, it was with the expectation that she was the one who would strive to satisfy *him,* in the bedroom in particular. After all, she was now one of the richest women on the planet. Where was the gratitude?

"I'm getting a chill," she said after a while. "Think I'll go inside and have Frederick light a fire. Join me?"

"Yes, of course."

He stood up and whistled. The shaggy, bear-like dogs raced across the lawn with astonishing speed. They sat at his feet, looking sweet and obedient, their pink tongues wagging.

"See?" Sterling told his wife triumphantly. "No trampling."

———

An interviewer once asked Sterling why he loved space exploration so much. Why he'd sunk the bulk of his fortune as a Big Pharma magnate into building a private version of NASA.

Of his four unmanned launches to date, two had ended disastrously. The rockets, intended for future journeys to Mars and beyond, had burst into fireballs long before reaching orbit. Undaunted, Sterling immediately vowed to press on, no matter the cost.

The reporter for a business magazine wanted to know why.

"Why do you persist? It has to be costing you billions. That's a high price, even for one of the world's richest men."

Sterling nodded.

"It's not cheap," he said. "But we need to know what's out there. We need to know if we're alone, and if we're not, well, it would be the most significant scientific discovery in history."

The quote sounded noble, selfless even. The truth was far less inspiring.

While the Mars program garnered headlines, Sterling's space division, Galactix, had been quietly positioning itself as an exclusive airline to the stars. Also, *for* the stars, as in the Hollywood variety.

Private flights into near space had already begun, using sleek Galactix shuttles. Longer trips to the Moon would follow. Resorts on the lunar surface and in orbiting space stations would come next.

The possibilities seemed endless – for whoever claimed them first. And Sterling had greased his way to the front of the line with both promises and bribes.

NASA had already given its consent to the ventures, signing exclusivity agreements that drew little fanfare. Sterling was currently negotiating with other space-minded countries, including China, Russia, Japan, India and the United Kingdom. Guaranteeing handsome payoffs, he was on the verge of an interstellar monopoly.

Within 10 years, he estimated, he'd double his fortune. In another decade after that, he'd be the wealthiest man in the galaxy.

That part of the plan always made him happy.

———

"Darling, wake up."

Sterling opened his eyes and saw his wife gently shaking him by the shoulders. He'd fallen asleep in front of the fireplace. The thick logs had burned down to embers.

"How long was I out?"

"A couple of hours. I didn't want to wake you, but we should go to bed. It's late."

Rubbing his eyes, Sterling yawned. He saw that his wife had changed clothes, perhaps hoping to create a romantic moment. She was wearing a feathered gown and the diamond necklace he'd given her for her birthday last year.

They walked side by side up the twisting grand staircase, then down the long hall past the other bedrooms until they reached the master suite.

Ashley unclasped the necklace and handed it to her husband. She said nothing. It was one of their frequent after-party rituals.

Tonight's glittering strand was worth a cool quarter-million, but it was one of the least extravagant pieces in her dazzling collection, which would have been the envy of Tiffany's. There were dozens of golden rings, bracelets and tiaras worth small fortunes, each adorned with the finest – and largest – gems available.

Sterling removed his shoes and padded barefoot through the immense, marble-floored bathroom, with its built-in spa, his-and-her dressing rooms and gold-plated fixtures, toilet included.

There was an elaborately framed wall-to-ceiling mirror next to the clawfoot tub and the billionaire walked up to it and pressed a hidden button.

With a high-pitched whir, a panel in the ceiling opened and the mirror rose into it until only the bottom showed, revealing a secret door. Sterling tapped a series of numbers on the keypad. With several loud clicks, the vault-like, reinforced steel door unlatched, opening inward.

Sterling stepped into the spacious paneled room and headed for the museum-quality backlit display case in the center.

Arrayed around him was a custom clothes closet, built-in refrigerated compartments with enough food and water to last several weeks, an entertainment system, pull-out beds, a stocked mini bar, two semiautomatic handguns with ammunition, extensive security camera feeds and an emergency communication system.

There was also a large safe, recessed into a wall, where gold bars, cash and other valuables were stashed.

The walls, ceiling and floor of the safe room were bulletproof and blastproof. The independent ventilation system equipped with viral-screening filters was tamperproof. The room was solar-powered with a backup generator in case the grid went out.

If things ever got really bad, there was an escape hatch concealed under the carpet that led to a tunnel running under the house and ending in a natural cave at the water's edge. There, a pair of shiny yellow WaveRunners waited in the shadows, unseen by people on passing boats.

The safe room had never been tested because there had never been an emergency, but Sterling paid handsomely to have it built. It seemed like a cool thing to do at the time. Also, prudent.

Now, years later, the novelty had worn off. His wife had a lot of very expensive jewelry that couldn't be kept in a box on the dresser.

Yawning again, Sterling returned the necklace to its resting place on the top level of the case. As the mirror slowly slid back into place, he brushed his teeth. Then he traded his dress shirt and pants for silk pajamas and climbed into bed with his wife.

"What time are we leaving for Belize?" Sterling asked.

"After your breakfast. No rush."

"Am I really the devil?"

"What?"

"The devil. That's what Caprice thinks."

"No, darling, you're just rich."

Pleased, Sterling nodded. Then he reached up and turned off the light.

CHAPTER
NINE

THE GUARD DIDN'T see them coming.

How could he? He was fast asleep on his chair in the shack that controlled the security gate at the Sterling estate.

When the men in black, their faces partially concealed with neck gaiters, crept up to the booth a couple of hours before dawn, the guard might have spotted them on the monitors – if he'd been conscious. Power to the island, along with phone lines, had been cut – but many of the mansions, Sterling's included, had emergency power systems.

Langston looked at the snoring security man and grinned. So far, so good. He slapped duct tape over the uniformed man's mouth and watched, with some amusement, as his eyes opened wide in surprise.

Seconds later, he was tied into a fetal position and left on the floor of the shack. One down, four to go.

There were a dozen men in the group that came ashore in dinghies, easily avoiding detection. They'd been personally trained by Langston over the past 11 months, aided by a tabletop mock-up of Billionaire's Row and his patient surveillance of the biggest mansions and their security teams.

The Sterling estate was the biggest prize, and the first to draw their attention. If it could be seized, the others would quickly fall.

Careful to avoid motion detectors and other sensors, the invaders headed next to the annex where the rest of the live-in security team had their quarters, complete with a swimming pool, billiards room, lounge area and small, but well-stocked, armory.

With any luck, three of those men would be sleeping. The fourth would be inside the immense main house, making rounds, according to Langston's notes.

He cut the secondary power feeding the annex, then waved for his commandos to pick the lock on the rear door as quietly as possible. They slipped inside one by one, drawn down a hallway by loud snores. They'd trained for a fight, respecting the fact that several of the targets were former Rangers and Green Berets.

Disappointing Langston, there was no firefight. No punches or combat knives thrown. Within 10 minutes, the stunned security detail was gagged and bound.

Glancing at his watch, Langston knew the last security man would be completing his checks and returning to the annex in a few minutes, eagerly handing the responsibility over to someone else.

Right on time, the man arrived.

He was wearing sunglasses despite the darkness and an earpiece that at this hour was connected to no one. The gun in his holster was covered by a tailored suit.

As he swiped his access card and entered the annex, Langston was waiting. Approaching from behind, he pressed the barrel of his Glock against the back of the man's head.

"Don't move," Langston whispered, removing the shocked man's gun. "You're done for the night."

For the next hour, the men in black moved silently from mansion to mansion, meeting no resistance. Not a single shot was fired. Not a single alarm, silent or otherwise, was triggered. It went down so smoothly that even Langston was surprised.

Eleven deeply embarrassed security men were rounded up and stuffed into the back of a truck. They were dropped off on the city side of the bridge with a warning: "Don't try to return. Turner Island is closed."

With private security eliminated, the invaders were free to roam the docks and helipads, sealing off the island. Once that was accomplished, the only tasks that remained were to clear all the homes and businesses. The school gymnasium was being set up to house the bulk of the islanders.

Caprice, who arrived shortly after sunrise, was delighted with the success of the high-stakes operation. While they had the element of surprise, the raiders were largely unarmed, and the men they were confronting were supposedly highly paid security operatives with impressive resumés.

"We'll soon have full control of the island," Caprice told Langston. "You've done well, my friend."

"Thank you, Father." Nothing pleased him more than praise from the man he admired most.

"Now we just need our friend Stone," the preacher said with a smile.

———

The first thing the detective noticed was that Joey was right about the tent city. Gone. Not a single asshole in sight.

The encampment had been a fixture on the corner for years, a real pain for the city and the department. But now, inexplicably, everything had been erased. Not a trace remained that it had ever existed.

"I'll be damned," Mike McCoy whispered.

He steered the unmarked sedan, a beige four-door Buick, down the block, inching past the church. Then he saw the trucks. A neat row, like Joey said.

Probably nothing. Just some movers.

He pulled over and studied the situation, taking a long sip of his lukewarm Dunkin Donuts coffee – black with extra sugar. There was nothing suspicious about the vehicles at first glance, other than the fact that they were all idling. But the men milling around caught his eye.

They didn't look like Bible thumpers. Not at all. These people were all dressed in black. And they looked lean and locked in.

McCoy watched as the men filled the cabs of the trucks, which began backing out onto the deserted street, one by one. As they passed his car, the detective ducked, hoping the tinted windows would keep out prying eyes.

After the last truck passed, McCoy glanced at his watch: 6:25, about an hour after sunrise. He took another gulp of coffee, then began following at a discreet distance.

Where you boys headed?

He knew, though. His guess was confirmed 15 minutes later, as the convoy began rumbling down the floating bridge, bound for Turner Island.

If it had been a long trip, McCoy would've radioed in his whereabouts. Follow standard procedure. But he could see the misty outline of the island ahead and decided he'd wait and see.

As he approached the roundabout that formed the only way in

or out, a man in a fluorescent orange vest and hard hat suddenly appeared. He waved at the Buick, commanding it to stop.

McCoy hit the brakes and rolled down his window.

"I'm sorry, but you'll have to turn around," the man said. "There's been a gas leak and we're preparing to evacuate."

The detective craned his neck and saw a crew starting to erect a barrier, effectively closing the road. Sandbags were being pulled out of the trucks he'd been following.

Sandbags? For a gas leak? And what does the church have to do with it? Nothing is adding up here.

Frowning, McCoy flashed his badge.

"I'm going to need to look around," he said.

"Suit yourself," the man in the vest shrugged. "You can pull over there."

A few minutes later, McCoy was checking the contents of one of the trucks. His eyes widened when he saw the crates. Each bore stenciled warning labels for "high explosives."

A shadow suddenly fell over him. He turned to see a large man with dark, sunken eyes.

And then a fist like a concrete block swung his direction.

CHAPTER

TEN

STONE CURSED as he raced down the bridge, trying to make up time. Even sober, he hated getting up this early.

For all his faults, though, he'd never missed an appointment with a source. Not once. He had to build trust, often in a hurry, and the best way to do that was to act as professionally as possible.

He'd been thinking about what Caprice said. That he was the only reporter he really knew. He wondered how that could possibly be true, given the fact that People's Oasis and its pastor had been written about extensively. Some would say exhaustively. The New York Times had recently done a glowing profile, calling him "the new face of religion." Whatever the hell that meant.

It occurred to Stone that the priest was referring to their candid counseling sessions and that made his skin crawl. He was normally so tight-lipped about his feelings, so guarded emotionally.

He arrived five minutes late, which wasn't bad considering his still-shaky condition. A man in a construction vest saw the laminated PRESS card on the dash.

"He's waiting for you," the worker said, which struck Stone as odd.

How many people knew he was coming? "There's an area to park ahead."

Stone grabbed his notebook and stepped out of the newly retrieved Subaru. It was a warm, humid morning, typical for early July. Bees were hovering over the white daisies surrounding the chiseled WELCOME TO TURNER ISLAND sign that greeted motorists.

Waiting, a few yards away, was Caprice. He was wearing casual clothes: short-sleeved linen shirt in khaki, fashionably faded Levi's, newish running shoes. The ever-present clerical collar was missing. He looked more like a guest at a beach party than a priest.

They shook hands. Stone, lacking his usual infusion of caffeine, skipped the niceties.

"Okay, I'm here, like you wanted," the reporter said flatly. "What's up?"

Caprice smiled, expecting the brusque reception. "Take a look around and tell me what you see."

Stone did as he was told. Workers were putting the finishing touches on a makeshift barricade, with rows of sandbags backed by heavy landscape timbers. A long banner was draped in front, declaring WORSHIP GOD, NOT MONEY!

"You're blocking the highway? Why would you do that? A lot of commuters are going to be pissed."

"Undoubtedly. But you're missing the big picture, Jeremy. Look again."

The reporter's eyes swept across the shore to the shopping district. Frightened people were in the streets, being led somewhere by steely men in black. Despite the distance, he could hear men shouting and women screaming.

"Oh my God, you're taking over!" Stone exclaimed. "You're taking over the island."

"That's right," the pastor said. "As we speak, teams are going from building to building. In a matter of minutes, we'll have complete control."

"*Why?* Why are you doing this?"

"To send a message, draw a line in the sand. At long last, take a stand. Dire circumstances sometimes require extreme measures. This is one of those times."

"You're doing this for homeless people? For addicts? You could testify before Congress. March on Washington. Lead a goddamn hunger strike. Why *this?*"

"Not only the homeless and the addicted, Jeremy. We're doing this for the entire underclass. The working poor, the unemployed, the millions and millions of people living below the poverty line, watching their car get repossessed as the rich get richer. We're fighting for them."

"So, you picked Turner Island because of what it represents?"

"Exactly."

"What are you going to do with the people? Kill them for their sins?"

Caprice pursed his lips. "God will handle that part. I'm merely His messenger. I can assure you that we don't *want* to harm anyone."

Stone looked over at the business district again, saw more wide-eyed people being forced out of buildings.

"Those people in the streets don't look very happy. They look terrified, in fact."

"That will pass – when our intentions are known. When the world hears our message."

Stone laughed bitterly. "When's that gonna happen? Because any minute now, the police will bulldoze your flimsy barricade and stick you all in jail."

"Perhaps, but not right away. The authorities will try to negotiate a surrender first. They won't risk the lives of rich and powerful people, and the longer the standoff goes on, the more our message of economic justice will resonate across the globe. The haves and have-nots will at long last have a reckoning."

"Good luck."

"We don't need luck, Jeremy. We need you."

"Oh really."

"You haven't noticed that there are no journalists on the island other than yourself? No TV crews, no photographers. Only you. I've given you the exclusive of a lifetime. And all you have to do is what comes naturally: Report about what happens here. I promise not to interfere with your reporting or censor your dispatches. Every day at a specific time, we'll have cameras set up to broadcast live. All you have to do is tell the truth."

Stone shot the pastor an icy look. "No thanks, do it yourself."

"Ah, but they won't believe me. Not at first, anyway. But you … you're the incorruptible journalist, a professional news-gatherer with no vested interest in the outcome of the situation. No discernable bias."

"No matter what I say, they won't believe it. They'll think I'm a hostage or something."

"Don't underestimate yourself. I chose you for a reason."

"You play therapist and now you think I owe you?"

"Not at all. I'm just offering you an opportunity, a golden one at that."

"And if I refuse?"

"Then you'll have tossed aside the biggest story in the country, perhaps the world. Is that something you're willing to do? Isn't your career on life support as it is?"

"Fuck you."

"When we talked a few months ago, you craved another chance to prove yourself worthy. Your tears and desperation seemed genuine. Jeremy, I'm giving you that chance. Don't blow it."

"Can I leave?"

"Anytime you wish," Caprice said. "But you won't be allowed back. It's a one-time-only invitation."

———

Sterling lowered the Wall Street Journal, a paper he had flown in at considerable expense. He sipped his cappuccino, adorned on top with a foam heart. Then he plucked a few red grapes from the fruit bowl and popped them in his mouth.

Ashley was brushing her long hair at the table again, a habit he loathed, but he said nothing. She looked at him with those Bambi eyes and smiled. Songbirds were singing outside. It was a bright, sunny start to the day, with clear skies and calm waters.

"Lovely morning," she said.

"Mmm," he intoned from behind a wall of newsprint.

Neither of them noticed that the security detail that usually greeted them in the morning wasn't around.

The dogs suddenly began barking, prompting Sterling to go to the window and look across the rear lawn. The mastiffs were at the helipad.

"Probably nothing," he said.

Just then the helicopter collapsed, falling slowly on its side like a tired elephant.

"What th—?" Sterling began, but then his wife screamed.

He turned to see an enormous man standing next to her.

"We've been waiting," Langston said in his eerie monotone. "Father didn't want us to wake you."

"Security!" Sterling yelled. *"Security!"*

Langston grinned. The panic in the billionaire's eyes pleased him greatly.

"There's no one here to protect you," he told the spaceman. "The island is ours."

———

Adelaide Stevens, 81 years young, was on her phone, breaking the first rule of mindful meditation: No phones.

Weathers, who was leading the session at Tranquility Cove, gave the silver-haired offender a withering look.

"Oops," the affluent Australian said, sliding the device back into her bag. "Grandchildren, am I right?"

"Poor dear," the woman next to her said. "They're so needy, aren't they?"

Having lost the attention of the class, Weathers decided to end the session a few minutes early.

"We'll meet again next week," she announced, as the pastel-colored yoga mats began being rolled up. "Remember to leave your devices at home."

They were filing out, gossiping as they went, when a tall, slender man with shoulder-length hair entered the spa. She didn't recognize him at first without his flowing robes.

"Good morning, Cicely," he said.

"Oh, it's you, reverend. Hello."

She heard what sounded like a scream and rushed by the pastor to see what was going on. She tried to step outside, but Langston suddenly appeared, filling the doorway. He was huge up close. The menace etched on his face was unnerving.

She wheeled around and saw Caprice studying her carefully.

"Please come with us," he said. "We have a lot to talk about."

ISLE
OF THE
RICH

CHAPTER

ELEVEN

ACROSS THE NEWSROOM every TV was on, tuned to the stunning breaking news. Work stopped. Clacking keyboards went silent. Everyone froze in their tracks – even the intern fetching coffee.

After the first alert went out, Burgess, who was still at home, immediately phoned the metro desk. "Send a full team to the scene. Reporters, photogs, videographers, anyone else you can think of," he demanded, but they were already on their way.

As the ME raced to the paper hours earlier than normal, he received an update that made him curse. The team had been stopped about a mile out. Police were setting up a perimeter a safe distance from the barricade. Nobody was allowed to pass. The photographers with their extra-long lenses struggled to see anything.

As the satellite news trucks began to arrive, patrol boats peppered with snipers formed a ring around Turner Island, sweeping away a handful of curious kayakers. Police drones equipped with video cameras buzzed and swooped. A 12-member SWAT force with full body armor and assault rifles took up positions on the bridge.

A war zone in the middle of a bustling metropolitan area. And nobody, it seemed, saw it coming.

People watching at home couldn't believe their eyes. As the siege unfolded, some cried. Others shook in fear. Would we soon be hearing about mass executions and a body count? Was this another 9/11 in the making?

"What the heck's going on, Sally?" Burgess asked. They were in his office, watching in disbelief as scenes of chaos played out in grainy loops on cable TV. "Is it terrorism?"

Graphic images of ordinary people running for their lives in The Commons filled the screen. Betters shrugged.

"Nobody has claimed responsibility yet, and the police are mum," she said. "There must be a hundred cops out there, and a bunch of armored vehicles. I wonder when they'll go in."

Hopefully, not soon, Burgess thought. He knew a great story when he saw one, and this yarn was unfolding on his goddamn turf. A gift from the news gods, landing right at his feet.

Burgess had been at the helm for eight years, only to fail to grasp the holy grail: a news Pulitzer. That deficiency in his resume bothered him immensely. The paper's coverage last year of a storm that caused massive flooding and home-crushing mudslides, two horrifying mass shootings and a scandal involving shady real estate appraisals won some honors, just not the top prize. And time was running out. Retirement was two years away.

Betters glanced at her phone, then the TV. "Mayor's office announced that they're sending someone to try to negotiate, but I don't see any sign of that happening yet."

"These things can take time," Burgess said, wishing out loud. "Remember the takeover of that urban neighborhood during the police shooting protests? They held the police precinct, for God's sake, but the mayor refused to storm the barricade. It took weeks but ended peacefully."

"Yeah, I remember. When the police finally went in they found an organic community garden and some pretty murals. Somehow, I don't think that'll happen here. Seems awfully serious."

"Wish we had a source on the inside."

Betters grimaced, wondering why she hadn't mentioned Stone earlier. Maybe she was hoping he'd simply disappear and stop being her personal burden. Maybe she was hoping that a journalist who drank away his career would put the final nails in his own coffin.

She took a few moments to psych herself up, then blurted: "We do, I think. I mean, *maybe*."

"*What?* Who is it?"

"Stone."

"Our Stone? You've got to be kidding."

"Nope," she said thickly. "He went to the island this morning to meet that pastor from People's Oasis, the homeless advocate. Something about getting pitched a 'big scoop.' I thought it'd be a waste of time. He did, too. But he drove out there anyway."

She glanced at her watch. "About an hour ago, right before shit began to fly."

"So, you're telling me that one of our investigative reporters is smack dab in the middle of whatever the hell is going down on Turner Island? Possibly at the invitation of the man leading it?"

"Looks like it."

Burgess clasped his hands together and smiled. *A gift from the gods, alright.*

"Have you spoken to him?"

"I've been trying. He's not answering his calls, and his voicemail is full. I have no way to reach him."

By itself, that wasn't unusual. Not for Stone. He often ignored calls and texts from editors while working a story, considering it meddlesome interference. But he had to know the grave magnitude of the situation unfolding around him at the moment. Surely, he'd reach out.

She checked her phone again and shook her head.

"Crap," Burgess said, frustrated. "Maybe the terrorists seized it. Maybe he's under duress. … Well, we'll just have to play this by ear. Let's create a story budget and meet in the conference room in an hour, okay?"

Betters nodded and left the office, feeling a bit dizzy. It was shaping up to be a massive story, and Stone was a huge wild card. Less than 24 hours earlier, she'd hoped to shed the emotional baggage of a troubled reporter. Now his life could be in peril.

Where the hell was he?

———

The Chronicle's top editors didn't have to wait long for an answer.

Exactly two hours into the invasion of Turner Island, Stone suddenly surfaced amid the maelstrom. Live on TV.

Looking uncomfortable and unkempt, the journalist stepped up to the camera, a mic clipped to the lapel of his tan corduroy coat. He took a deep breath that made his chest rise.

"I'm Jeremy Stone, an investigative reporter at the Chronicle," he began. "By now, you're no doubt aware that Turner Island is under siege. The island has been taken over by a group that espouses radical changes in the way this country deals with poverty, drug abuse and homelessness.

"The leader of the group, the Rev. Charles Caprice of People's Oasis Church, invited me here today so that I can inform the outside world about what is transpiring, and I've freely agreed to do so. Every day until the situation is resolved, I will report on the conflict, using the church's broadcasting system. Caprice has personally promised not to interfere with my fact-gathering or censor the reports in any way."

Stone glanced sideways at someone hidden from view.

"We'll soon see if that pledge is honored. Despite the dangerous situation here, I want to assure everyone that I'm not a hostage or prisoner, although my phone has been seized and I've been asked not to contact people on the mainland.

"Here's what I know so far: Two hours ago, Caprice's followers began rounding up every person on the island and taking them to undisclosed locations. I am not aware of any major injuries.

"As you probably know by now, the floating bridge leading to the island – the only route in or out – has been cut off. Boats and helicopters have been scuttled, preventing anyone from leaving. From what I've been able to see, however, no homes or businesses have been damaged or destroyed. Power on the island was cut off early this morning, but it has since been restored.

"Caprice told me earlier today that he chose Turner Island because it is one of the wealthiest enclaves in the world. He intends to hold the island in order to raise awareness about the chasm between the haves and have-nots in our society.

"As for the residents being held, he has only stated that he wishes them no harm. The people holding the island do not appear to be armed.

"I'm being told to wrap this up, so I guess that's all for now. This is Jeremy Stone, reporting from Turner Island."

Flabbergasted, Burgess and Betters exchanged glances.

"I can't believe our luck," the ME said. "The biggest story of the year, and we have the only reporter on the scene. The longer the standoff goes, the better it'll be. We'll have to increase our press runs."

Betters gave him a sour look.

"I thought you'd at least be concerned for Stone's welfare. You and I both know that if he says one critical thing, Caprice and his goons will come down on him hard. His life may be at risk, and you're talking about press runs."

"You're right," he said, chastened. "But there's nothing we can do, so let's do the next best thing. Clear the cover and as many inside pages as you can."

———

Upps came running into the mayor's office, panting from the exertion.

"Sal! Sal!"

Pucci emerged from the attached conference room, where he'd been upbraiding a couple of policy aides.

Upps was catching his breath, mopping sweat off his head with a handkerchief. "We've got a problem," he said.

The mayor sat in the high-back leather chair behind his desk, his preferred place in which to receive troubling news.

"What is it? Spit it out!"

"Caprice has led a band of his disciples to Turner Island. They're taking it by force."

Pucci couldn't believe what he was hearing.

"That's preposterous," he snapped. "Impossible. Where are you getting this from?"

"Turn on your TV!"

The mayor grabbed the remote on his desk. The TV in the cabinet where he kept his booze flicked on, tuned to CNN.

Footage taken from a news helicopter showed the manned barricade and people running in the streets. File photos of Caprice filled the upper right corner of the screen.

WEALTHY ISLAND OVERRUN, TERRORISM NOT RULED OUT read the chyron stretched across the bottom.

"Jesus Christ," Pucci uttered, eyes bulging.

The mayor gathered himself after a few moments. To his chief aide, he barked, "Get everybody here ASAP! Police, fire, emergency services, even the goddamn National Guard. Notify the board of supervisors and the governor. And start preparing a statement."

"Yessir!" the aide said before dashing out.

Upps flashed one of his wry grins.

"Well, there's good news, Sal," he said. "At least we know Caprice won't be running against you."

———

Caprice clapped when Stone signed off.

"Bravo, nicely done," the pastor said. "Apologies for cutting you off there, but when it comes to dispatches from the island, less is more."

Stone sat heavily on a stone ledge and groaned.

"This doesn't feel right," the reporter said in a low whisper. "It's like a damn hostage video. Nobody will believe a word."

"You underestimate your sincerity," Caprice said. "They'll believe because *you* believe."

"I want to leave."

Caprice looked stung. "You can leave if you wish. But do you really want to walk away from the assignment of your dreams? As we speak, your little message is being relayed to millions of people around the world. You're on the verge of becoming a media sensation, Jeremy. You're going viral."

"I don't care. You're the one who wants to make a splash, not me."

"Yes, that's true. I do have a message to send, one preaching love and compassion and equality. It requires the support of some important people with homes here. I'll be having dinner tonight with Hugo Sterling and Cicely Weathers. Please join us. It may help you decide whether to stay or go."

Stone looked up. He'd very much like to know if Weathers, the chief spokesperson for the island, and Sterling, one of the world's richest men, had been harmed in any way. Perhaps forced to sit at Caprice's table.

"Okay, I'll be there," he said.

"Excellent."

"Am I free to walk around?"

"Certainly – with an escort, of course."

"*Of course*," Stone echoed sarcastically. "Can I have my phone back? For reporting purposes."

"Afraid not. But you're not alone. As a precaution, we've collected everyone's devices; laptops and tablets, too. We have to control the on-island narrative if we're going to truly be heard. Right now, we're the bad guys, the invaders. But that will change and hopefully soon. In the meantime, I'll have Langston bring you writing supplies."

Stone frowned.

"Gee, thanks."

TWELVE

AS CAPRICE WALKED through The Commons, past Dolce & Gabbana, Cartier, Chanel and House of Bijan, past the galleries with their curated collections, past the Gucci bags, Ferragamo shoes and Le Chocolat sweets, it all seemed familiar.

He'd never stepped foot on Turner Island before, but he didn't have to. For the first 20 years of his life, he was rich.

His family lived in splendor on Sardinia's fabled Costa Smeralda, a stretch of azure waters and powder-soft white sand beaches. The Caprices made their money in real estate, specifically in luxury hotels, and Charles grew up in the sprawling penthouse of the most exclusive five-star resort on the coast.

As a boy and only child, he received the finest education, with tutors flown in from around the world. He had his own spotted pony at the age of 7. Scuba lessons by the son of Jacques Cousteau and a private reef to explore at 10. At 13, for his birthday, he was given a Formula 1 race car and a track built to Grand Prix specifications on which to practice.

His French-Italian parents, Andre and Camille, were kind but rarely at home, constantly traveling the globe in search of the next big resort property. Charles was raised by a nanny and butler who pampered him tirelessly, surrendering to his every whim. By most definitions, it was a splendid life.

Yet he threw it all away.

He had been groomed to take over the company, Caprice Luxe Ltd., sitting in on executive board meetings at an early age and receiving regular briefings on everything from expansion plans and site development to union-busting strategies. Yawns and eye rolls didn't stop his father's minions from their appointed task of preparing the young protégé.

As a bright-eyed 17-year-old, Charles was sent off to a prestigious East Coast business college, where he excelled, rising to the top of his class. His parents were thrilled. Andre bragged about his son to anyone who'd listen.

"The company is in good hands," he'd say with a broad smile. "Very good hands indeed."

But midway through his second year, Charles radically changed course. He began studying theology instead.

Andre didn't interfere at first, telling his wife that their son's redirection was a "passing fancy." Still, Andre couldn't help but notice that Charles had managed to free himself of all financial support. He began working in restaurants, clearing tables and washing dishes. A seasonal job in construction blistered his hands and scorched his skin. He got himself a modest studio apartment and slept on the floor.

He loved all of it. The sacrifice of comforts, the living month to month without a safety net. But was it just an experiment? An act of rebellion? Even he couldn't say for sure.

Then one day, during a rare home visit, he told his shocked parents that he wanted to become a priest. And not only a priest, but a Jesuit who takes a vow of poverty in order to be closer to God.

Andre told his son enough was enough.

"We've waited. We've been patient. But it's time for you to complete your business studies and prepare to lead our family business," the elder Caprice said at the dinner table.

"I don't want to spend my life reaping profits," Charles protested. "Can't you see? I don't want to be like you. I intend to devote my life to helping others, especially the poor. In the past two years, my eyes have been opened to all the suffering around us."

"That's noble, son," his mother said. "But all this religious talk, it's a flirtation. Your true calling is to become a brilliant businessman like your father."

"How do you know what my calling is? I mean, if anyone should know my destiny, it's me and me alone."

Andre shook his head.

"You won't be a priest. I forbid it!" he barked. "Poor people are poor because they're lazy. Get that through your thick head!"

"I'm sorry, father. I truly am, but I will choose my own path."

"If you persist, there will be no support from us and no inheritance in the future," Andre said, his face flushed red. "Nothing. Zero."

"Always about money," Charles said soberly. "There's so much more to life than that."

Months passed, and then a certified letter came. It was from one of the family's lawyers, threatening to cut Charles out of the will, an inheritance worth north of $800 million, if he didn't immediately end his religious studies and resume his proper business education.

The terse demand made Charles cry. His father couldn't even manage to write the words himself.

He held firm, even after his parents severed all contact, essentially abandoning him as a lost cause. He moved to the United States, eager to distance himself from his former life. He became a priest, learned the rituals and practice at several churches, then struck out on his own in a radical way.

Caprice found working the streets in a big city, ministering to the homeless, to be both exhilarating and exhausting. In a touch of irony, he also put his long-suppressed business acumen to work.

At the age of 26, he founded People's Oasis with $500 in cash donations. Within five years, it would grow into a powerful nonprofit with six shelters, five detox centers and a $9 million budget.

But it wasn't enough. Instead of helping thousands, he wanted to improve the lives of millions. And not just in one city, but around the globe.

The only question was how.

———

"Bless you Father, for what we are about to receive."

Stone watched in astonishment as Caprice uttered the prayer and servants under his control laid platters of food on the table, enough for a banquet: Creamy potato soup, followed by roasted pork loin, mushroom tagliatelle, mixed greens with shaved radish and warm whey bread.

Across from Stone sat Sterling and Weathers. Both looked as anxious as he was. They were gathered inside one of the island's newly shuttered restaurants, a chic French bistro named Le Jardin.

At the head of the table, Caprice smiled. He tipped his wine glass toward Sterling.

"I want to thank my illustrious guest for the loan of his chef," the priest said with a musing twist to his voice. "Langston, will you join us?"

The bodyguard hesitated briefly, then filled a chair next to Stone.

"I apologize sincerely for having to be so … *forceful*," the reverend said, eying his guests. "I trust no one was harmed. I've given strict orders."

"What's the meaning of this, Caprice?" Sterling bristled. "How dare you round us up like cattle."

Stone noticed Langston's hand slowly slide to the holster on his side. It was a subtle movement, unseen by the others. He faced the pastor with a blank expression, ready to spring into action.

Caprice sighed. "A necessary step, I'm afraid. There was no other way to swiftly take control of the island, I assure you."

"Where is everyone?" Weathers asked. "Where did you take them?"

"They are safe. Most are housed in the school gymnasium, others in the theater and private homes. They are comfortable. Meals and bedding have been provided."

He tossed a casual glance at Stone. "You may speak with them later if you wish," he said.

To Weathers and Sterling, he added: "This is Jeremy Stone of the Chronicle. I've invited him here to report on what's transpiring. I've pledged my full support, with no interference. The story needs to be told."

"Yeah, right," Sterling scoffed. "You're really going to let a reporter run around when the entire island is locked down? Give us a break."

The way the billionaire said it, it did seem far-fetched, Stone thought. More surreal than real. But so was the invasion itself, and that was definitely happening.

Caprice sliced a tender piece of pork. "Please eat," he said cheerfully. "Food should never be wasted."

"Bring it to the school," Weathers said carefully. "Please."

"Of course. Whatever is left."

Stone had no appetite, but rather than risk upsetting Caprice and his muscular right-hand man, he took a bite of bread. The other guests followed.

They ate in silence for a few minutes. Then Sterling dropped his fork with a clatter and demanded answers.

"Enough of this charade. What do you intend to do with us? And why can't we remain in our own homes?"

"We're all innocent," Weathers put in. "We've done nothing."

Caprice's gold eyes glowed.

"You've been moved out of your mansions, *everyone has*, in hopes that you can think more clearly. Hugo, Cicely, you attended my last Sunday service, listened to my sermon on wealth inequality, the great cancer eating away at this nation.

"Surely, One Percenters such as yourselves knew a reckoning was coming – that someday you'd be asked to pay your fair share. Someday, all the tax loopholes and legal dodges would catch up to you. That day is today. The bill, so to speak, is due. And through the power of the Lord, I intend to collect."

"Total horseshit!" Sterling bellowed, and this time Langston drew his weapon. He placed it on the table with a thud.

Caprice looked over at his protector and shook his head.

"I'm establishing a fund to benefit the needy," he told Sterling in an even tone. "Every inhabitant of this island, including yourself, will be invited to contribute. I'd like you to kick things off, Hugo."

Stone sat there, astonished. Was Caprice really intending to play the part of Robin Hood in this drama, taking from the rich and giving to the poor? If so, it was a good thing he didn't leave.

Things were getting interesting.

Sterling glowered at the priest.

He wasn't used to being threatened or intimidated, tactics he himself often employed. He had an army of aggressive, high-priced lawyers on retainer – a salivating pack of wolves ready to rip apart anyone who dared stand in his way.

"Over my dead body," he snarled.

"Oh dear. Let's hope it doesn't come to that," Caprice said. "Dessert anyone?"

CHAPTER
THIRTEEN

FALLONE CREPT along Billionaire's Row, avoiding roaming patrols. He appeared calm, his breathing steady, but his heart was pounding. His forehead was damp with sweat.

Minutes earlier, he'd watched in disbelief as men in black swarmed over the boulevard and its grand estates, asserting control. For what purpose, he had no idea, but he suspected it had something to do with money. Lots and lots of money.

Violating the curfew, he'd been sleeping at the Andrews-Weathers home since spotting the van prowling around, feeling anxious and unsettled. It had nothing to do with the fact that Andrews was at another conference, leaving his wife alone, he told himself.

He was relieved when Cicely left the home before 6 a.m. to take a pre-dawn walk and prepare for her morning meditation class, thinking he'd overblown the whole damn thing in his head. As McCoy had said, nothing bad ever happens on the island. That was indisputably true, so why couldn't he shake his sense of dread?

Fallone watched from his ground floor bedroom window as Cicely left the estate on foot in her sneakers and lilac yoga pants, disappearing into the dark.

Debating whether to try to get some more sleep, he heard what sounded like a scream. He returned to the window and did a double-take.

The older couple who lived next door were being pushed into the street, still in their night clothes, silver hair askew.

What's going on?

Moments later, he saw the men in black turn his direction. He ducked behind the curtains so they couldn't see him, but he knew they'd be coming. It was the last home on the row.

Fallone had a decision to make. Should he try to resist, perhaps surprising the intruders as they broke in? Or should he flee and assess the situation?

He sneaked another peek and saw at least four shadowy figures approaching. No, he thought, there's too many of them and he had no gun. Cicely didn't want any in the house, a prohibition he'd respected.

Opening his door a crack, Fallone could hear the men moving around inside the house, searching for the occupants. He cursed under his breath. His cellphone was in the small backpack he often wore when making the rounds, left in the foyer in plain view. It was certain to be searched and seized.

He quietly opened a rear window and lowered himself to the ground. Then he dashed to an old oak and crouched behind its thick, gnarled trunk.

Watching in horror, he saw people up and down the boulevard being forced into the street, some in tears, pleading for their lives, others in a state of dull shock. It was fortunate, he thought, that Ernesto and the other workers at the Andrews-Weathers home weren't due to arrive for a couple of hours.

It was a full-scale invasion of some sort, he surmised. But why on Earth would a priest and his followers do such a thing?

It was dire thoughts of Cicely being harmed that spurred the security man to make his way to the business district, using hedges and trees as cover. The sun was rising, making him feel more exposed, but he had to move quickly. Her life was in danger.

Fallone was about to cross a cobblestone driveway when two of the men in black suddenly appeared. He ducked behind a bush dotted with scarlet flowers as one of them lit a cigarette.

"Did you see the size of that safe room?" the smoker asked.

"Man, it was a big one," the other man said, laughing. "Huge."

"Waddya think's inside?"

"Gold, diamonds, cash. You name it. These bastards are stinking rich."

"Yeah, they should call this place Treasure Island."

"Ya got that right, brother. And it's ripe for the taking."

The man with the cig stubbed it out with his foot. "Don't get excited. Remember Langston's orders."

"Yeah, yeah. But a guy can dream, can't he?"

"Dream on, brother. At least we're sticking it to 'em."

"At last. Come on, let's finish searching the place."

Fallone heard laughter and fading footsteps, then peered around the corner to make sure they were gone. He wondered if they were mercenaries hired by the church or radicalized followers.

Either way, they seemed dangerous.

———

McCoy opened his eyes in a small room, hands bound behind his back.

He had been placed on a bare wooden chair in the middle of what appeared to be a shed, hastily cleared of its contents. His gun was gone. Dried blood stained his chin from a broken nose.

Outside the door he could hear voices. Men talking in hushed tones. They were wondering what to do with him. Whether it was best to dispose of the problem by dumping it in the sea.

He heard them jump to their feet, then another man with a deeper voice arrived. Seconds later, the door swung open.

"Detective," Langston said brightly. "Have a nice nap?"

The enormous man stepped behind McCoy, who tensed, fearing another clubbing. Instead, his hands were freed.

"Just a few questions and we'll send you on your way," Langston said. The men behind him, disappointed, shook their heads.

McCoy said nothing.

"What brought you to the island?" Langston asked. "Who tipped you off?"

"Nobody. You people are super suspicious-looking."

Langston balled his right fist and McCoy tensed again, but the blow never came. Instead, the interrogator leaned in and whispered. "I wouldn't have answered the question, either."

He paced the room for a few moments, then said in a normal voice: "Does anyone know you're here?"

"Loads."

"You radioed in?"

"Of course."

"You're lying."

"Whatever."

"I can tell. I've always been good at knowing."

"Good for you."

"The truck you were searching. What did you find?"

"Oh nothing."

"What were you looking for?"

"Toilet paper. This place doesn't have any. Are we done?"

"Yeah, just one more thing," Langston said. He coiled his arm and punched the prisoner in the face with enough force to knock him to the floor.

As fresh blood trickled down his face, McCoy looked up and seethed.

Langston recognized the bloodlust in the man's eyes. It was something they had in common.

"I can see you're too dangerous to keep around," he told McCoy.

The detective saw the gun on the big man's hip. He braced himself for a bullet, but Langston had other plans.

"Take him to the barricade and release him," he told the guards. "Maybe the police snipers will do us a favor."

CHAPTER

FOURTEEN

THE MAYOR PACED the hastily assembled war room, filled with equal measures of outrage and angst.

Early attempts to negotiate with the radicals hadn't fared well. An envoy from City Hall approached the barrier waving a white handkerchief but was forced to flee under a hail of stones. To some observers, the response seemed biblical.

Nobody, Pucci included, had a way to reach Caprice, the purported leader of the takeover. For unknown reasons, he didn't own a phone.

As standoffs go, this one was nuts. No declared demands. No obvious motive. Just a protest banner on a makeshift barricade. Was it a fleeting political demonstration or something far more serious and sinister?

"Carl, what do we know?" the mayor, sounding flummoxed, asked Police Chief Carl Winterbrook.

Winterbrook, who was about to turn 68, had recently announced his decision to step down by the end of the year. He rose from his seat at a long table lined with emergency services officials, political leaders and the commander of the National Guard unit based outside the city. Agents from Homeland Security and the FBI were on their way.

"According to our intel, which mainly comes from drones, everyone on the island at the time of the takeover has been rounded up and taken to secure locations, where they are being guarded," the chief said.

"Private helicopters and vessels appear to have been disabled, preventing anyone from leaving. The bridge barrier is manned by up to a half-dozen men. Others are fanned out in groups of two or three, patrolling the shoreline."

"Are they armed?" Pucci asked.

"Hard to say. There may be rifles, but the images so far aren't very clear. Caprice's bodyguard has a carry permit. That's all we know at this time. That said, it would be prudent for us to assume that they do, in fact, have weapons."

"And why's that?"

"Because it would be foolish to erect a barricade and have no way to defend it," Winterbrook said. "Rocks won't stop armored vehicles and SWAT teams."

"Why are they doing this? Anybody? Speak up."

"My guess is that it's about sending a message," said Jon Snowden, the bespectacled emergency services chief. "I'm told the church has the ability to broadcast live remotely, accessing its public access channel via satellite. For the last couple of years, they've also been streaming events on their website."

"Anything from them on the web about the island?"

"Not yet," Snowden replied. "Just replays of sermons."

Pucci was trying to wrap his head around the tenderloin church being able to afford sophisticated broadcasting equipment. But wasn't he responsible for that?

"Obviously, they were planning this for some time," Snowden continued. "I think the reverend was waiting for the right time — when he could preach to a mass audience."

"You're saying Caprice is willing to go to prison in order to lecture the world about evil rich people?" Pucci asked, incredulous.

"Yes. He's been warning for years that drastic action was coming. Nobody took him seriously, all of us in this room included."

The National Guard leader cleared his throat noisily. Like Winterbrook, Oscar Dinwittie had arrived in full uniform.

"We need to move quickly," he said, military boots tapping under the table. "The sooner, the better. We don't want them digging in. Or worse, harming innocent people. The longer we screw around, the greater the chance of a massacre."

Pucci glanced anxiously at Upps, who was leaning casually against a wall.

"We want to avoid bloodshed, of course," the mayor said, drawing a snort from Dinwittie. "I know this preacher. Yes, he's a radical, but to my knowledge he's never espoused violence. What about that reporter who's on the island? Can we use him to get to Caprice?"

Winterbrook shook his head. "We have no way of contacting him either. Editors at his paper are cut off, too. Looks like we're stuck. We'll have to wait for them to reach out to us."

"Damn," Pucci muttered. "Any thoughts, Upps?"

The strategist rubbed his chin as eyes around the room drilled into him.

"Maybe we go old school," he said. "Deliver a letter to Caprice. On paper, mayor's office letterhead. The men at the barricade will have no choice but to pass it along."

"Good idea," the mayor said, brightening. "What should we say?"

"Tell the preacher you want to talk man to man," Upps said. "From everything I know about Caprice, he won't be able to resist."

———

Turner Academy, the island's elite private grade school, certainly looked regal enough.

Ivy covered the stone façade, which had been built to look much older than it was, in a New England sort of way. In the center of the front lawn, a hedge had been pruned into the shape of a wolverine – the school mascot.

The academy capped enrollment at 100 in order to boast an enviable 5-to-1 student-teacher ratio. Other perks included napping rooms, a cafeteria featuring an award-winning chef, and regular playground visits by baby goats, alpacas and llamas.

Stone didn't care about any of that. He just wanted to get inside and talk to as many people as he could. Find out what was really going on.

Soon after the tense dinner party, Langston left the reporter at the front door.

"You've got one hour," he grumbled.

"Father didn't set any time limits."

"Yeah, but I don't trust you." He tipped his oversized head toward a pair of dour sentries. "One hour. Knock and they'll let you out, take you to your quarters."

Stone hadn't even thought about where he might spend the night. Things had been happening so fast. He was still riding high on adrenalin.

"And where's that?" he inquired.

"You'll see."

Langston disappeared into the night, headed in the direction of the barricade. When Stone turned around, the school's massive front door was open.

The reporter made his way to the gym that doubled as an auditorium and performing arts center. It was now filled with people and row after row of cots covered in blankets and pillows. It resembled a Red Cross relief center more than a jail.

A hush fell over the room when Stone entered. Noticing, he waved his ever-present notebook.

"I'm a journalist!" he shouted. "I'm here to find out what's going on."

An elderly woman rushed up to him, grabbed the sleeve of his coat.

"What have they done to Cicely?" she asked in an Australian accent.

"She's fine. I just saw her," he told her, and the woman nearly fainted in relief. Stone helped her back to her cot.

"I'm Jeremy Stone with the Chronicle. What's been going on?"

"Thank God you're here. I'm Adelaide. Moved to the island after my second divorce, 20 – *no, 21* – years ago. Anyway, we were doing our meditation at Cicely's when the ruckus started. Out of nowhere, these men appeared, ordering everyone to line up. They took our phones!"

"Mine, too. Go on."

"Yes, yes. Well, the scary men put all the people from The Commons here – except Cicely, of course. All morning, more and more people came – taken right from their homes. Poor dears were scared silly. All of us were."

"Was anybody hurt?"

"I- I don't think so. But you should ask Henry." She stabbed a bony finger toward a distinguished-looking man with a silver goatee. "He's a retired doctor. Runs the clinic to keep busy."

Stone finished the interview and excused himself. Heading toward the doctor, he wound his way through the maze of cots, trying not to further alarm anyone.

A freckled mop-haired boy who looked to be around 10 suddenly appeared, blocking his path.

"I'm Frankie," he said. "You can talk to me if you want."

"Hello, Frankie. Are your parents here?"

"Naw. They're overseas somewhere. They left me with Petra. She's our housekeeper."

"I see. And where's Petra?"

The boy shrugged. "No idea. They took her someplace else. But that's cool. I like being on my own. I know all the ways in and out of this school. All the hiding places, too."

"Well, take it easy. The guys in charge seem dangerous."

"They can't catch me. Let 'em try!"

Before Stone could respond, Frankie was gone, sprinting through the gym. He could see a couple of the men in black watching and shaking their heads. Clearly, the boy had already made an impression.

Stone found the doctor sitting ramrod straight on the edge of a cot, eyes shut.

"You're the journalist?" he asked without looking.

"Yes."

"We're all being held against our will. Write that down."

"Has anyone been injured? Mistreated in any way?" Stone's pen hovered over the lined pages of his notebook, ready for a juicy quote.

"Not to my knowledge, but the experience itself is terrifying, of course. That's why I'm doing my controlled breathing exercises. Reduces stress, you know."

He finally opened his eyes and shook Stone's hand.

"Henry Cavill, M.D. They raided my clinic as I was performing a prostate exam on a patient. Quite embarrassing, as you might imagine. The hoodlums ordered us into the street and the next thing we know, we're brought here."

"What have the conditions been like?"

Cavill smiled. "Well, there are worse prisons. It's Turner Academy, after all. What the school didn't have, they brought in. Somebody planned this thing – whatever it is – very well. Looks like they were expecting a long stay."

"Why do you say that?"

"Look over there," Cavill said, gesturing at the far wall. "Enough canned food and toiletries to last weeks, maybe months. Only wish they'd brought Scotch."

The doctor was right about the supplies. Stacks of cartons and boxes rose halfway up the wall and extended roughly 20 feet.

Stone checked for eavesdroppers, then leaned in, lowering his voice.

"Is there a way to communicate with the mainland? Get a message out?"

Cavill thought for a moment.

"There's a small radio station on the north shore," he whispered. "Strictly for locals; lacks the power to even reach the mainland. If you could get inside, however, there's all kinds of equipment. They've locked us down, but if they're letting you roam around …"

"Stay safe," Stone said. "I'm going to talk to a few more people. Then I'll see what I can do."

———

Fallone was watching.

The security man had managed to climb up to the roof without being seen. Now he was observing the captive people below through a skylight.

He'd scanned the gym several times. As far as he could tell, Cicely wasn't there.

Then Fallone saw the man enter the gym. He couldn't hear what he said. But he saw him waving a notebook and got the gist of it.

Incredulous, he watched as the journalist calmly interviewed a handful of anxious detainees. *In the middle of a siege.*

He decided to follow the reporter from a safe distance until he could get him alone, find out where Cicely was being held.

Once safely on the mainland with her, he'd tell McCoy everything he knew. Admittedly, it wouldn't be much.

He still had no idea what Caprice and company were up to.

———

Bloodied and bruised, McCoy made his way across the bridge.

He still had his badge, which he held over his head. With each step, the police line drew closer. He wondered how many snipers with itchy fingers had him in their sights.

When he could see the black helmets of the SWAT guys, McCoy started yelling.

"I'm a cop! I'm a cop! Don't shoot!"

There was no response, which made things worse. McCoy began to sweat, fearing for his life. Then, a dozen steps from the police line, a bullhorn came to life with a burst of static.

ON THE GROUND! *NOW!*

McCoy did as he was told, lying face down on the asphalt. Seconds later, officers rushed out and yanked him up by his collar.

They saw the badge. And the dried blood.

"Jesus, he's one of ours," one of them said.

CHAPTER
FIFTEEN

IT WAS CURIOUS that the place they picked to house Stone was the doctor's cottage behind the clinic.

Cavill was a widower with three daughters, now in their 50s and scattered around the country. Stone deduced those facts by examining the many framed photographs displayed throughout the house, including the one attached to the obituary of his wife, Hazel.

The house was charming but cluttered, with century-old oak floors, a rock fireplace and a laddered library. There, overstuffed bookcases lined three walls. Along the fourth sat a large antique desk buried under a mountain of printouts, medical journals, magazines and newspapers. The copy of the Sunday New York Times at the peak of the messy Everest had been printed five years ago and was yellowing on the edges.

The good doctor, it appeared, had failed to do any substantial cleaning since his wife's death from cancer seven years ago.

Upstairs, in the master bedroom, the closet was so jammed with boxes the door couldn't close. They held tokens from Cavill's many overseas adventures.

Stone browsed the treasures, finding an engraved ceramic stein from Bavaria, a reproduction of a Zulu warrior shield and a colorful hand-woven hat made in Peru. Sprinkled among the items were snapshots of the Cavills, in tourist garb, smooching and holding hands. The images made Stone smile.

As he was wrapping up his home tour, he discovered a hidden bar tucked under the stairs. He stood there, eyeing the stock of expensive booze, for several minutes. Maybe longer.

Strangely, he heard the whiskey bottle calling out.

Jeremy, is that you? Have a drink, m'boy. A lovely, lovely drink.

Stone took a deep breath, willing his frozen feet to thaw. A pair of lead crystal glasses were resting on the bar mat, easily within reach.

The fingers on his right hand unfurled.

That's right. Take a glass and pour. Fer old time's sake.

"I- I can't! Stop it!!"

Stone covered his ears. He forced himself to back away, step by step. It felt like pulling shoes out of wet concrete.

He shut the door and pressed his back against it, breathing heavily.

Was this why he was taken here, to this particular cottage? To test his resolve? See if he'd fall through the ice?

Well, if anyone was watching, he very nearly did.

He returned, shaken, to the library. Desperately needing a diversion from the siren's song, he cleared off the desk and pulled out his notebook. He began flipping through the narrow pages, circling key facts and quotes. In the morning, he'd be making his second live report to the outside world. He felt a familiar feeling – an elusive quest for perfection.

As he began writing the script for his stand-up, he was interrupted by a tapping at the window behind him.

Stone was jarred by the sight of a man staring at him through the glass. He had a friendly but determined face and was wearing a blue T-shirt and jeans, not the signature black of Caprice's followers.

"I'm Fallone," the man said in an urgent whisper. Stone raised the window as quietly as he could so as not to alert the sentry on the front porch.

"Joey Fallone. I handle security for Cicely Weathers. Mind if I come in?"

He didn't wait for an answer. In a flash, he was in the library, looking around. He saw the notebook and its scrawled entries.

"You're the reporter."

"That's right, Jeremy Stone. How'd you find me?"

"Followed you from the school. I'm trying to locate Cicely, get her outta here. Do you know where they're holding her?"

Stone shook his head.

"No clue, sorry. But I was with her earlier this evening, and she's fine."

Fallone looked relieved.

"Why isn't she with the others, at the school?"

"There's some kind of crazy plan to siphon off the island's riches and give it to the poor. Every billionaire and megamillionaire will be asked to contribute. I think they're all being held separately so they can be squeezed."

"This is Caprice's doing?"

"Yeah, and his minions."

Fallone's trained eyes scanned the room. "Hey, is there a phone here somewhere?"

"No, they've seized every device they can. They've thrown a net over the island."

"Damn."

"There's one possibility. The man who lives here told me that the local radio station has all sorts of electronics. You may be able to rig something."

"Why didn't I think of that? They have a place off the beach. Maybe Caprice's goons haven't noticed yet."

"What are you going to do?"

"Call the cops," Fallone said, halfway out the window. "Help them take this damn island back before people get killed."

———

Just two days had passed, but Jeremy Stone mania was already in full bloom.

His live daily reports were breathlessly watched by people around the globe, like Caprice had anticipated. TV networks immediately rebroadcast the dispatches. Endless analysis and commentary followed. Major newspapers and wire services quoted Stone extensively. Podcasts devoted to the drama began sprouting like weeds.

The journalist's earnest face was projected onto the enormous screens at Times Square and even the legions of tourists in the area paused to listen.

Across Manhattan at the United Nations, the Security Council discussed the situation. There were regular briefings at the White House and 10 Downing Street. Russian propagandists wasted little time, saying the seized island signaled the beginning of the end of "corrupt Western capitalism."

The Chronicle found itself in the eye of the hurricane. Because Stone himself couldn't be reached for comment, the press corps descended on his employer, eager to know anything about the fearless reporter trapped on an island overrun by dangerous zealots.

Of course, the Chronicle was profiting by the drama at the same time.

The press run was now at 200,000 copies – more than double the normal volume. Trucks had to be added to the distribution fleet. Special editions were in the works, featuring teams of writers. It was as if the only story going on was the invasion of Turner Island.

And so, on the second day of the standoff, Burgess and Betters found themselves in a conference room at the paper facing dozens of journalists from around the world. Microphones and cell phones lined the entire length of the table.

"What is Jeremy thinking right now?" a reporter for The Times of India asked. "Is he scared?"

"I don't think so," Burgess answered. "He's been an investigative reporter for a long time now. He knows how to handle himself in tough situations."

Other questioners wanted to know if Stone was single, what he did in his spare time, whether he liked cats or dogs better. Betters rolled her eyes more than once.

In a bizarre turn of events, the troubled journalist on the brink of getting canned just a few days ago was now a hero.

The ME was delighted.

First, he was granted the story of his dreams. Then the reporter working it was becoming a media sensation. He only hoped that the Chronicle's glowing profile of Stone, in the works since the second hour of the standoff, would be published ahead of the pack. Every major outlet and publication, it appeared, was pursuing one, including Time, People and Der Spiegel.

A BBC reporter asked Burgess if Stone had any prior experience in broadcasting.

"None at all," he said. "But he's doing pretty well under tough circumstances, I'd say."

The Associated Press asked whether Stone appeared to be brainwashed.

Betters took that one.

"No, we think he's doing what comes naturally: reporting the news."

"How can we trust what he's saying?"

"Nothing he's reported so far has been disputed by authorities," Betters replied. "I've been his editor for six years. I trust him to do his job, and that's to report accurately and fairly."

The AP reporter frowned. "You trust him, even after the libel suit?"

It was Betters' turn to scowl. "*Especially* after the libel suit," she snapped.

Another reporter asked, quite seriously, whether Stone might be communicating a secret message through his blinks.

"You mean, like, by Morse code?" Burgess asked, causing some in the room to titter. "No, not to our knowledge."

The press conference ended with both Burgess and Betters feeling relieved.

Nobody had mentioned the drinking.

———

The letter from the mayor's office was brief and to the point.

"Dear Rev. Caprice," it began. "As mayor, it has fallen upon me to negotiate an end to the ongoing standoff on Turner Island.

"I am deeply concerned about the welfare of the innocent people on the island. As a man of God, and one who has never espoused violence as a means of solving deep-rooted problems, I trust that you also wish to avoid escalation that could result in bloodshed.

"It is my understanding that the takeover of the island was motivated, at least in part, by your desire to deliver a powerful message about wealth inequality. That message has been delivered, loud and clear, I can assure you.

"I am now offering to meet with you in person in order to find a peaceful solution. Due to the urgency of the situation, your prompt response is appreciated.

"Sincerely, Mayor Salvatore Pucci."

Caprice was finishing his daily meditation when the envelope was delivered by one of his disciples.

The pastor read the brief letter twice.

"Negotiations are about to begin," he told Langston. "As we expected."

CHAPTER
SIXTEEN

THE FBI AGENT arrived just as the call came in.

Pucci, seated at his desk, put the rogue priest on speaker. The police chief, city attorney, National Guard commander and head of the board of supervisors were gathered on chairs, set in a half circle. Behind them, Upps was wearing out the carpet, treading back and forth.

"This is the mayor speaking," Pucci said, as calmly as he could.

"Mr. Mayor, it's good to talk with you again," Caprice said.

"Please, call me Sal. I take it you received my letter."

"I did indeed. You wish to negotiate."

"That's correct."

"So, go ahead. *Negotiate.*"

Pucci glanced at the FBI agent, who was busily jotting notes.

"Yes, well, I'll get straight to the point then. What are your intentions with the civilians you've taken hostage? Can you guarantee their safety?"

"'Hostage' is such a loaded word. It implies that people have been taken prisoner and that we are the enemy. Quite the opposite, actually. People's Oasis is the ally of all people, rich and poor alike.

We are merely putting the richest of the rich on notice: They must do more to alleviate poverty and suffering. Surely by now you've realized that Turner Island, a symbol of wretched excess, is the new pulpit from which we are preaching."

"We've been watching the Stone reports like everybody else. But what about the safety of the people there?"

Caprice sighed. "They are safe and being treated well, I assure you. That will continue – if you allow us to finish God's work without interference."

"God's work?"

The FBI agent scribbled more notes. Dinwittie shook his head sourly.

"The message we are delivering to the masses," Caprice explained. "When we are certain that it's been heard, we will remove the barricade and peacefully surrender. Everyone here will be free to go about their lives."

"Reverend, how long do you figure this will take?"

"Days, possibly weeks. There is no way to be precise about such things. *Spiritual* things."

"Stone reported today that the wealthiest residents of the island are being asked to contribute to some kind of fund for the poor. Is that true?"

"That is correct. The first deposits have already been made."

"And they're doing this without coercion?"

"The only coercion they face is from within: A guilty conscience."

"Reverend, please understand that I am under enormous pressure to end this standoff. Like *yesterday*. I can give you another 48 hours. After that, the police and military will likely take drastic measures."

A silence, thick as molasses, hung in the air.

"Reverend? Reverend, do you understand?" the mayor asked.

"There's one other thing I can guarantee, Mr. Mayor," Caprice said finally. His usual melodic tone was gone, replaced by something darker.

"What's that?"

"Any attempt to storm the island will end catastrophically. Ask McCoy. I believe he knows."

"I'm sorry, but…"

"If you wish to talk further, it will happen here, on the island. Just you and me. Good day."

Caprice hung up.

"What the hell just happened?" Pucci said, looking exasperated. "And who's this McCoy?"

Winterbook, the top cop, spoke up. "Mike McCoy, one of our detectives. A veteran. He tailed a convoy of trucks to the island, but before he could radio in he was captured … and roughed up."

"And I'm hearing about this now?" the mayor asked, looking pissed.

"Sorry, Sal. We've only just finished the debriefing. He believes there were crates filled with explosives in the trucks. By now, the entire island could be rigged to blow the moment we move in."

"Jesus."

Sam Smythe, the FBI agent, cleared his throat, drawing the attention of the room.

Trained as a profiler, Smythe had come from the D.C. headquarters with crucial experience the others in the room lacked. He'd been involved in two prior prolonged standoffs involving religious cults. One ended peacefully; the other disastrously, with a mass suicide.

"They let McCoy go precisely because they *wanted* us to know what he saw," he said. "I believe they think it'll buy them more time."

"It's all crap," Dinwittie interjected. "If explosives were being placed in locations across the island, the drones would have picked it up. We'd have known about it."

"Not if they were careful," the chief said. "Not if the bombs were placed indoors, out of view."

Pucci glanced at Upps, who shrugged dramatically. The mayor was on his own.

Fortunately, Smythe had an idea.

"McCoy said a former cop on the island, a security man named Fallone, tipped him off about the trucks," the agent said. "I've reviewed all the drone footage to date with McCoy, and he's convinced that Fallone hasn't been captured. If he's free and able to move around the island, he's probably searching for a way to contact us. McCoy will likely be who he reaches out to first."

Pucci scratched his head. "So, what are you saying?"

Smythe smiled.

"Give it another 48 hours, like you told the preacher. There are a lot of preparations to make."

——

Bridget and Barry sensed an opportunity.

While technically under house arrest in the Airbnb, the power couple immediately began plotting an end game in which they would prove themselves invaluable to the radicals and thus survive the situation. Possibly with another notch in their belts as high-priced fixers.

The plan hinged on convincing the leader of the invading army to accept their help in persuading the captive billionaires to contribute willingly and substantially to the anti-poverty fund. Once the bank transfers started, they'd have the leverage they needed to get off the island.

It wasn't an ideal situation, with the reverend in charge of the takeover being a wild card, but Bridget and Barry didn't lack for confidence.

They wrote a note to Caprice and weren't surprised at all when they were granted an audience, downstairs in the spa.

With Langston by his side, the reverend greeted the well-dressed pair cautiously.

"I'm all ears," he told them.

"Thank you," Barry said, looking sharp in his designer suit. They had decided that he'd be the opener and she'd close the deal. "We're pros at negotiating solutions to messy problems. We get celebrities and high-profile business people out of sticky situations all the time.

"We saw on TV that you've established a fund and are seeking to have the wealthiest people on this island contribute. My wife and I can help you do that."

Caprice looked amused. "Really. How so?"

"By persuading them that it's in their best interest to do so. Contributions would likely be tax deductible, yes, but more than that, from a public relations standpoint, they would be viewed as caring about the plight of the underclass."

"Even if they don't."

"Exactly. A true win-win."

"And how much money do you intend to seek from these people?"

Barry hadn't anticipated being asked that question. He was simply hoping to get as much as he could, on a case by case basis. He glanced nervously at his wife.

"Probably a few million dollars each. Depending, you know, on their income levels, investment portfolio, that sort of thing."

"A token," Caprice said bitterly. "You would accept crumbs on my behalf."

Things weren't going well. Bridget waded in, intent on saving the day.

"What Barry is saying is we'd ask each billionaire to contribute a proportionate share. That way they could feel that their contributions are fair," she said. "It would make things much easier."

"I see," Caprice said. "And what would *your* contribution be? How much?"

"Um, no," Barry stammered. "I don't think you understand. We're saying we can help you by *arranging* the contributions. We're not billionaires, not even close."

"What did your PR firm gross last year?"

"Um, I can't remember."

"Does $550 million sound right?" Caprice said, waving a sheet of paper. "That's what this business article says."

"There's so much overhead in a big firm. The net is a far smaller number," Bridget argued.

"Well, let's not quibble," Caprice said. "One million dollars from each of you seems 'proportionate,' to use your word. Arrange that, and we can talk further. Langston, please return them to their apartment."

"Wait! We're trying to help you!" Barry protested as he was pushed toward the stairs.

Bridget seemed stunned, caught off-guard for one of the few times in her career.

The reverend wasn't as easy to manipulate as she'd thought.

———

Since the island was overrun, Weathers found herself grappling with powerful, conflicting emotions.

While fearful of what may happen to her friends and neighbors and seething over the audacity of the "invasion" itself, she couldn't help but feel pangs of sympathy for the reverend's cause.

As the head of The Commons governing board, she was abundantly aware of Turner Island's staggering wealth. Also, its ugly secret: Few people gave back. Few gave a hoot about the poor.

She included herself in that category and it filled her with shame.

Sure, she and her husband donated generously to worthy causes, such as the children's program at the island's public library branch, the youth soccer league and the beautification fund, which included the award-winning floral arrangements in the hanging baskets. But the gifts were always fully deductible – they checked with their accountant before writing the checks – and they also benefitted personally from the largess.

There was another thing that now bothered Weathers. Another realization. The couple had expected recognition for its contributions. The thank-you plaques hanging in their den. "Cicely Weathers and Darren Andrews" etched on a forever stone in the courtyard fronting the addition to the Opera House on the mainland. Glowing mentions in various monthly newsletters. Applause at the annual black-tie banquet.

What had they done for the poor? The ill? The hungry? Nothing, Weathers thought glumly.

Absolutely nothing.

She'd been housed in a loft above the Gucci store and she now traced ovals in the carpet, pacing and thinking.

Just a week ago, she and Darren were in the city, headed to a new restaurant that had received glowing reviews for its creative cuisine. They came across a man with a frayed cardboard sign on his lap that read, "ANYTHING HELPS. BLESS YOU."

The man was sitting on the sidewalk, his back against a chain-link fence. His face was dirty, his clothing torn. There was a hole in the sole of one of his boots. When he saw them, he smiled, revealing a missing front tooth.

"Disgusting," Darren spat under his breath.

Refusing to make eye contact, he took Cicely's hand and pulled her along, making a wide arc on the sidewalk.

"Have a good day," the man called out.

Cicely, struck by the man's kindness, paused to fish in her purse for a few dollars. Darren stopped her.

"He'll only blow it on booze or drugs," he said. "Don't waste your money."

Recalling that moment brought tears to her eyes. She was an heiress and yet never in her privileged life had she given selflessly to those less fortunate than herself. Maybe that explained her fascination of late with People's Oasis and its message. Maybe that explained the painful guilt she was feeling.

She sat down at a table and composed a note. Darren wouldn't like what she was doing, he'd likely throw a fit, but she was past worrying about such things.

When she was done, she folded the page and handed it to the man stationed outside her door.

It read:

Dear Rev. Caprice,

I've come to the realization that you are right about one very important thing: The 'haves' must do more to lift up the 'have-nots.' I intend to contribute to your fund. I am also willing to share my decision and thoughts with the others, if you think that might help.

Please be merciful in dealing with the people here. A message as powerful as yours takes time to sink in. It certainly did for me.

Sincerely,
Cicely Anne Weathers

SEVENTEEN

BEFORE

"HOW ARE YOU feeling today, Jeremy?"

Stone was in his thin hospital gown and slippers, staring out a second-floor window in one of the clinic's spartan, ultra-sanitized day rooms. Caprice was perched on the edge of a folding chair, looking concerned.

The patient, ghostly pale, shrugged. "Okay, I guess. *Better.*"

"That's good. Your withdrawal symptoms are less severe than expected. The nausea, the shakes – that should all be over soon."

Another shrug.

Stone could see the encampment below. Homeless people buzzing in and out of tents of various sizes and colors. He wondered if he'd be joining them soon.

"Why do you care?" he muttered. "You're not even on the staff."

Caprice leaned back. "You're correct. I'm not one of the licensed clinicians, but I have been ministering to people facing difficulties for many years, and this facility is overseen by my church."

"Yeah, I've seen the brochure."

"So, you know you'll be transitioning to individual counseling and a 12-step program when you're feeling better."

I'm Jeremy, and I'm an alcoholic.

I'm also radioactive, having nuked my career. So, keep a safe distance.

Stone scowled. "Looking forward to it. Sounds like a blast."

The priest ignored the sarcasm. "I'd like to be your counselor. Would that be okay with you?"

Stone finally turned to examine his visitor. He was wearing a simple black jacket and slacks with a clerical collar. A plain silver cross rested against his chest. His soft brown hair brushed his shoulders. But it was his eyes – something different about them, the way they caught the light – that was the priest's most striking feature.

"Why so much interest? I'm just another bum trying to kill himself with booze."

"You're a special case, Jeremy. I've been interested in you for some time. I've read all your big stories."

"Why would you do that?"

"Because you have a gift, a very important one, and it would be a pity to waste it."

Stone shook his head. "Bullshit. I'm a fuck-up with a drinking problem, like millions of ordinary Joes."

The priest brightened. "I'm encouraged to hear that you recognize your addiction, Jeremy. That's a crucial step toward recovery."

"Yeah, yeah."

Stone began holding his trembling right hand. Caprice, noticing, rose to his feet.

"I'll be back around this time tomorrow," he said. "You should rest."

———

Stone's sessions with the reverend didn't start well.

There was something about priests and the selfless nobility of their work that made the journalist suspicious. Caprice's gentle compassion – a universe apart from his own unfailing cynicism – seemed almost theatrical.

But when the pastor's placid demeanor never wavered, Stone gradually lowered his emotional walls. He didn't fully trust Caprice, he never would, but he began revealing himself as never before.

"When did you know you were going to be a writer?" Caprice asked one afternoon.

Stone's physical appearance had changed. His cheeks regained some color. He sat up straighter and looked stronger. He glanced at the reverend, allowing himself a thin smile.

"Since I was a boy. When I was in fifth grade, I started writing these creative essays. The other kids were doing the basics. You know, What I Did on My Summer Vacation. I'd write these elaborate stories set in crazy worlds drawn from my imagination. The teacher loved them. She'd read them to the class. That was the start for me. I began devouring books – mostly fiction with a heavy dose of fantasy. Comic books and graphic novels, too."

"Why go into journalism instead of becoming an author?"

"I could have gone either way, honestly. I think journalism had more immediacy, more power to expose wrongs and that was pretty intoxicating. Sorry, wrong word."

Caprice smiled. "And you still love what you do?"

"Oh yeah. Despite … everything."

"You met your wife when you were a reporter?"

Stone's peaceful expression faded. "No, a few years before. I was in college in New York writing for the student paper and she was waiting tables at a pizza restaurant to pay her art school tuition. The moment I saw her face, those green eyes, the small cleft in her chin, I fell for her hard. You know how it goes."

"Actually, no, I have no idea," Caprice said with a wink, "but I hear it's nice. Tell me more about her."

"Jenny was the woman of my dreams. Smart, beautiful, funny when she wanted to be. I loved going places and doing things with her – it was always a good time."

He trailed off and Carpice saw tears.

"You never had children," the priest said after a while.

"No, Jenny didn't want any. She had a rough childhood, violent father and all that. She thought she was damaged goods."

"Was she?"

"Not really. I mean, yeah, in the sense that she had her emotional scars. When I met her she was on anti-depressants, had been since high school. Sometimes, she'd call off a date minutes before we were supposed to meet. 'You don't want to see me like this,' she'd say. But then I'd tell a coupla dirty jokes, make her laugh. We'd go ahead and get together, and it'd be great. I always thought her mood swings weren't that severe. I proposed after six months or so. She said yes. We were happy for a few years and then …"

A tear rolled down Stone's cheek.

"Then what?" the priest nudged.

"She became sick. Terminal. I was coming into my own as an investigative reporter, but the hours were crazy. Day and night, weekends sometimes. Before her illness, she complained, but I guess I didn't want to listen. Even later. Maybe especially later. Instead of tending to her, I'd put my stories to bed as if they were my children. I'd come home late and the house would be dark. Jenny would be asleep. I knew something had to change, I had to be there for her, but I was scared … "

Stone trailed off yet again. Caprice broke the silence with a whisper.

"So, you basically disappeared."

"Yeah, something like that."

"And one day, you came home to find your wife had taken her own life."

Stone's eyes widened. As far as he knew, only Betters and a handful of relatives knew those grim details.

Caprice continued. "She was crying out to you, but you were too weak to give her the emotional support she so desperately needed. And you've been blaming yourself for what happened ever since, punishing yourself at every watering hole in town. That's true, isn't it?"

Stone nodded solemnly, saying nothing.

His counselor, though, suddenly looked buoyant.

"Tomorrow we'll talk about your addiction," Caprice said. "I think we're making progress."

CHAPTER

EIGHTEEN

THE RADIO STATION was little more than a shack, isolated on a bluff covered with dune grass.

When Fallone cautiously approached, seagulls perched atop the metal roof looked down at him curiously. The only sound was the constant wind and slapping waves.

In the distance, he could see the outlines of what appeared to be police boats. They were probably sealing the perimeter, trying to contain the situation. Fallone thought that was ironic: Caprice and his followers were doing the same thing.

He'd been surveilling the shack for the past 20 minutes, and there wasn't a soul in sight. Time to make his move.

The small gravel lot attached to KXTI-FM – "Turner Island's Hit Music Station" – was empty. There were no signs of the roving patrols he'd been dodging since the invasion.

As he approached the entrance, though, his heart sank. The door was chained and padlocked. He'd need bolt-cutters to get if off.

Cursing, he retreated to a stand of spindly pines, curved by the elements. He was about to give up and resume his search for Cicely when a van drove up. It was a rusting VW Microbus straight out of the '60s, with hand-painted neon flowers on the sides.

A round man with a graying ponytail stepped out. To Fallone's astonishment, he went up to the door and removed the lock with a key.

"All those nasty things I've said about Hippies, I take it back," the security man said under his breath.

Barry Wizzander nearly had a heart attack when Fallone barged in minutes later to the tune of "Good Vibrations" playing on a studio monitor.

"Don't hurt me! Don't hurt me!"

"Stop screaming," Fallone said, putting a finger to his lips. "I'm avoiding the patrols. I assume you are, too."

Wizzander exhaled loudly. "Dude, I've been sleeping in Frodo the last coupla days. Laying low, you know?"

"Frodo?"

"My van. There's a bed in the back. Curtains, too."

Fallone grinned. "I'm Joey, nice to meet you. I'm an ex-cop who works private security out here."

"I'm Wizzander. People here call me The Wiz. I'm the one who keeps the music going. Also do some maintenance on Little Miss, cleaning off the bird shit mostly. That's our compact radio tower."

"Was that your lock on the door?"

The Wiz laughed, making his belly shake. "Yeah, figured it would keep the orcs from trashing the place if they thought it was like shut down or something. People got to have their tunes, am I right? Why are you here?"

"I need to find a way to contact the mainland. All the phone lines are down and everybody's cell has been seized. Can you help me?"

"I wish. Battery on my phone died like two days ago. The charger is at my house and I'm not going there, dude. Too risky."

Fallone looked around the tiny station. "No landline. … Can you cobble anything together from this gear? Make some kind of CB radio?"

"Sorry, I'm not a techie. I don't know what half this shit does. My job is to plug and play."

The security man thought for a long moment. "You say your charger is in your house?"

"Yeah, bedroom drawer. But it's on the other side of the island, dude. There'll be orcs everywhere."

Frodo. Orcs. Just Fallone's luck to be saddled with a Tolkien fan who freely mixed reality and fantasy.

"Lend me your phone, please," he said. "I've got to at least try."

With a shrug, The Wiz handed over the dead phone and jotted his address on a scrap of paper. Fallone stuffed both in his pocket.

He headed for the door, then stopped and turned around.

"Hey, get outta here quick," he advised. "They're sure to spot your van."

"Jus' need to load in another 24 hours," he said, tapping a stack of compact discs. "Classic rock, my man. Solid gold."

"Right. People got to have their tunes."

Fallone made it to the trees in a crouch, then spotted two men in black sprinting across the dune. They hadn't noticed him, it appeared. It was the van named after an adventurous hobbit that caught their attention.

They were headed straight for the shack, and there was nothing he could do.

Poor guy.

On the third day of the occupation, the music was about to die.

———

"This is Jeremy Stone, reporting from Turner Island."

There was only one thing more bizarre than being the only reporter on an island under siege, and that was watching his five-minute standups being replayed over and over. Hundreds of times a day on hundreds of channels across the planet. The planet part, he didn't know for a fact. But probably.

Eating the bland ham and cheese sandwich provided by his keepers, Stone stood in the living room of his comfortable jail and watched the TV news in amazement, flipping through the channels.

The anchors would toss video clips and sound bites to panels of "experts" for immediate analysis. Is Stone brave or foolish? Why would a serious journalist do a terrorist's bidding? Why isn't Caprice on camera instead? Have the upscale stores been looted?

There was no shortage of topics and sub-topics to explore, no matter how implausible or irrelevant.

"How courageous is Jeremy Stone?" asked one prime time anchor.

"He's clearly risking his life," said the guest, a former assistant director of national security. "He's reporting the news as honestly as he can, but how long will they let this go on? My hunch is not long."

The Chronicle had been devoting every front page slot to the standoff, running the full text of each Stone report. As bonus content, the paper published its glowing 10-page profile – headlined HERO SECOND TO NONE, complete with cute childhood photos. The libel suit and stint in detox were not mentioned.

News organizations competed for scraps, including interviews with Stone's proud grandparents, worried neighbors at the Tudor

Arms whom the reporter had never actually met, and unsurprised journalism professors, all of whom knew he was bound for greatness.

Stone watched all of this in disbelief. Being the center of the media universe was unsettling to say the least. He could understand why the world craved news from the island, but he couldn't fathom why he'd suddenly become a symbol of bravery and fortitude.

During actual wars, reporters embedded with troops showed far more courage. Bullets were flying around them. Some were killed. Christ, Hemingway was a World War II correspondent at the age of 45.

Stone was shaking his head when Caprice entered the room, giving the journalist a start.

"I told you they'd believe you," the priest said. "Every word."

"It's ridiculous. An embarrassing circus."

"You're giving them the truth. What they do with it is beyond your control."

Stone sneered. "I don't know what the truth is. Not really. Only what you *say* it is. This fund of yours, for instance."

"What about it, Jeremy?"

"You *say* it's to benefit the poor and yet you've provided no evidence to support that. You *say* people on the island are contributing voluntarily, but, again, I've seen nothing to prove it. Not a shred of evidence. You *say* the money will be distributed soon, but when and where and to whom exactly?"

"I know this is difficult to hear, but I need you to be patient. All of the answers to your questions will be revealed soon."

"Terrific. I'll be sure to mention that in my next report. Meanwhile, you keep me under surveillance and house arrest.

"You're being dramatic. I've not interfered with your reporting – your interviews. You are free to talk to anyone you wish, any time you wish. The men escorting you have been instructed to remain at a distance, so as not to hear what is said or obstruct in any way."

"What about the billionaires being housed separately?"

Caprice frowned. "What about them?"

"I'd like to talk to them privately, but you've kept their locations secret."

"Why is it important for you to see them?"

"Are you kidding me? Come on, man. They're the real reason all of this is happening. Sure, you're preaching about inequality and One Percenters, blah, blah, blah. But that's just talk, isn't it? If you can't get the billionaires to pump up that fund of yours, this grand scheme of yours falls apart."

Caprice laughed harshly. "I should have known that a jaded journalist such as yourself would have a hard time grasping what we're trying to accomplish here. The revolutionary nature of it."

"Yeah, well, I don't think Sterling is about to join the revolution."

Caprice sighed. After a few moments, he turned to face Langston, who had been standing motionless in the shadows. Stone immediately grew nervous, wondering if he'd pay a price for challenging the pastor.

"Langston, take our friend here to see Mr. Sterling tomorrow," the priest said. "And any of the others he wishes to interview."

———

Dinwittie walked down the row of Abrams tanks, never feeling more alive.

The liberal mayor and his equally woke friend, the governor, had finally granted him permission to begin organizing a strike force that would retake Turner Island and free the hostages. *And, God, did that feel good.*

He'd spent the past 24 hours drawing up a multi-pronged attack utilizing landing craft, tanks, armored bulldozers, attack helicopters and a few hundred of his most experienced troops. He estimated that the terrorists, badly outnumbered and outgunned, would be taken out within an hour. Probably within minutes.

After that, his force would quickly liberate the hostages, ending the standoff. He'd be hailed in the press as a military hero. Promotions would soon follow.

A soldier servicing one of the tanks popped out of a turret. He saw Dinwittie passing and saluted.

"Are we a go, Colonel?" he asked.

"Damn right we are, Sergeant. Damn right."

"Awesome!"

Dinwittie smiled as he entered the base headquarters and marched to his office. He was one day away from greatness. He could almost taste it.

The phone rang and he picked it up, hoping it was an update on the status of the landing craft he'd requested.

The commander cringed when he realized it was the mayor calling.

"I need you in my office tomorrow morning to go over the military response. We need to coordinate with the police and other parties," Pucci said.

Dinwittie wished he could tell the little man to go to hell. His plan was foolproof. He'd get the job done. That was a fact. And he didn't need anybody mucking it up.

"I'll be there," he said instead. "Looking forward to it."

CHAPTER
NINETEEN

ALL THE BILLIONAIRES had been removed from their mansions, and they weren't happy about it.

Especially Sterling.

He'd been taken to a loft above the island's only grocery store that, by the smell of it, had been used as a produce storage space. The bed they set up was too small; the linens too coarse. The only light was a naked bulb hanging from the unfinished rafters.

Worse still, there was no TV and all of his devices had been seized. He was completely unplugged, cut off. And it was driving him bananas.

The stern men would bring him bottled water, thin soup and white bread sandwiches twice a day, just like what he imagined they did in prisons. That thought made him angry. He was one of the world's most powerful men, and yet here he was, being treated like a common criminal.

All of his demands, and he repeated them multiple times a day both verbally and in writing, had been ignored by the high and mighty priest. He wondered if Caprice, the hypocrite, had moved into one of the commandeered mansions, possibly his own.

Was the hypocrite sleeping in his giant bed under the goose-down comforter, wrapping himself in the mulberry silk sheets? Was he helping himself to the fine wines in the cellar? The rare Napolean-era brandy he'd bought at auction for $250,000?

His angry daydream tumbled over to the valuables in his vault, worth many millions, and he found himself balling both fists.

When I get out of this hellhole, he'll pay. Oh, he'll pay dearly.

He was plotting his revenge when someone knocked at the door.

"It's Stone, the reporter," a voice called out.

Sterling groaned but opened the door anyway. He hadn't had a visitor in three days. Not even Caprice. And he was going stir crazy.

"I figured you'd come sniffing around," the billionaire said. "Welcome to my palace."

"Wow," Stone said, looking around at the unfinished space. A large fly buzzed around in lazy circles. "Smells like old fruit."

"Are you here to harass me even more? Ask me if I've seen 'the light?'"

"Not really. I want to get your take on what's going on and see how you're doing."

Sterling grunted. "What do you think? Caprice could have placed me on house arrest, but he dragged me here, to this awful place. Must have thought it was amusing."

Stone began writing in his notebook. "Or an object lesson on the value of giving?"

"I don't need any lessons from that fraud," Sterling snapped. "I have a pretty good idea what poverty is like. I'm a goddamn self-made man. I wasn't always rich."

"I don't really know what Caprice is up to, but I think he's separated the richest people on the island so he can work on you all, one by one. Maybe he thinks you can't focus in your mansions.

Maybe he thinks you're blinded by money."

"'Blinded by money?' You sound like him. Clearly, he's won you over."

Stone ignored the dig.

"Cicely Weathers has donated to the fund – $10 million," the reporter said. "I saw the letter she wrote, apologizing for not doing more sooner. She's offered to go around the island, encouraging others to do the same."

"Good for her," Sterling said icily. "I'm giving back in many other ways. I don't appreciate being held prisoner, forced to do his bidding."

"How have you been giving back, if you don't mind me asking."

"Through Galactix, I'm helping NASA explore the outer reaches of the galaxy, advancing scientific knowledge. That benefits *everyone*."

"Aren't you also profiting from those ventures?"

"Yes, of course. But that's the American way, how we built this country."

Stone paused to look closely at the billionaire. "You don't have a charitable foundation, like Gates and Buffet. You don't give away money like Carnegie did with the libraries. Why's that?"

Sterling started pacing the small room. He looked like a condemned man and a snarling beast combined.

"Those bleeding hearts? Screw them. I'm busy changing the world. The universe. What I'm doing is infinitely more important to humanity than studying mosquitos and stocking school libraries. Building a sports stadium, by the way, isn't really giving back, now is it?"

"If you're a fan, maybe it is," Stone said, grinning.

"Jesus Christ."

"Sorry, but what's wrong with the haves doing more to lift up the have-nots? More than anybody on this island, you're in a position to help. With the stroke of a pen, you could alleviate the suffering of thousands, perhaps millions."

"That's true, but then what? What happens five years from now, and five years after that, when those same people prove themselves incapable of making it on their own? When they keep demanding handouts?"

"Give more, I suppose. Offer free drug treatment, free tuition …"

"Until when? Until I'm as broke as they are? Is that what this is all about? Is that what Caprice really wants – to bankrupt all of the wealthy people in the world?"

Stone didn't know the answer. How could he? The verdict was still out: Was the priest Robin Hood or a con man with a collar?

Sterling stood in front of Stone, looked him in the eyes.

"He's a lunatic with a cross, and he'll be spending the rest of his life behind bars. Instead of questioning me, you should ask yourself why you're doing his bidding. Why were you chosen?"

Stone flinched. Maybe Sterling was on to something.

Maybe Caprice was pulling all the strings, making him dance to his tune. And he didn't even know it.

———

In the first nerve-wracking days of the occupation, Cavill took charge.

The doctor didn't necessarily want to. It's just that the community looked up to him, valuing his intelligence and unshakable aura of calm.

"Are they going to kill us?" a man asked him on the second day.

Cavill smiled in his reassuring way, a skill honed over many years as a family practice physician. "We'll be okay. Not to worry."

"How can you be so sure?"

"Because the people holding us are unarmed, the priest leading them preaches nonviolence and they've brought in enough food and other supplies to last a long time. Please, pass that along to any others who are frightened. It may help."

Soothed, the man nodded and walked away.

The next morning, Cavill approached the presumed man in charge of the ersatz detention center.

"I'd like your permission to take over meal preparation in the school kitchen," he said. "It will ease some of the tension by giving the people something to do. Plus, the nutritional value of the peanut butter and jelly sandwiches you're providing is minimal."

"There are too many weapons in the kitchen," Langston said with his usual blank expression. "Too risky."

"Then, by all means, remove the butcher knives and rolling pins. I'm only thinking about cooking a decent breakfast for a hundred: scrambled eggs, bacon, potatoes, buttered toast. … I'll recruit some volunteers to help."

Langston thought for a moment. He disliked having to prepare meals for the spoiled rich. If it was up to him, he'd toss them cans of beans. Make them drink out of a faucet.

Plus, with an entire island to control, his holy army was spread thinner than he'd liked. Having one less distraction, one less chore, wouldn't hurt. Maybe it made sense to make the detainees cook their own damn food.

Besides, Father would certainly approve.

"Okay, but under supervision," Langston said. "All cooking utensils will be checked out. If any go missing, I will hold you personally responsible, and that will not be a pleasant experience. Is that clear?"

"Perfectly," Cavill said. He glanced at his watch. "May we begin?"

The good doctor and a group of five volunteers whipped up a meal fit for a restaurant, which seemed appropriate since the school's kitchen was managed by an acclaimed chef. Fortunately for the chef, school was out for the summer and he was vacationing safely in southern France.

As Cavill expected, morale soared after the homey breakfast. The discovery of honey and preserves, plus an ample supply of ham, sausages and steaks in the kitchen walk-in – apparently intended for summer events and programs – only added to the excitement. The volunteer crew began brainstorming a meal plan spanning several days.

The doctor's plan to soothe everyone's frayed nerves seemed to be working.

Some of the islanders were watching soaps on the TVs brought into the gym and laughing. This isn't too bad, Cavill thought.

We'll survive this.

Then the national news broke in to show live video of a tank rumbling onto the bridge.

Cavill closed his eyes and steadied his breathing.

He wasn't a religious man, but if he was, he'd be praying.

———

It was The Wiz's house alright.

The giant peace sign in the front yard was a giveaway. So were the KXTI stickers adorning the porch planters, now overgrown with weeds.

A shaggy gray cat with blue eyes greeted Fallone, purring and rubbing against his legs. He checked the tag dangling off the collar and smiled. The cat's name was Gandalf. No further confirmation of the address was needed.

Fallone, who'd gotten pretty good at scaling roofs of late, saw an upstairs window that was partially open and found a sturdy rose trellis to climb. After a quick look around for anyone watching, he pulled out the screen and climbed inside.

It was The Wiz's messy bedroom, which resembled a college dorm with piles of dirty clothes, rock star posters and Dungeons & Dragons figurines – dozens of them in all different sizes. It looked like he was preparing to paint a winged creature named Bahamut, according to the box. "The patron and progenitor of metallic dragons."

Shaking his head, Fallone pulled open the nightstand drawer. The charger was there, just like the man said.

He went downstairs and plugged the phone into a kitchen outlet while he searched the fridge for something to eat. There was lumpy milk and moldy bread and little else. He pulled open a cupboard and was relieved to find an energy bar.

As soon as the phone got enough of a charge, he'd call McCoy, tell the detective everything he knew. With any luck, the police would be able to use the information to retake the island and free everybody, Cicely included.

He glanced at The Wiz's iPhone anxiously. The battery was at only 1 percent.

Seconds later, through a sheer living room curtain, he saw them. Three of Caprice's followers clad in black led by a hulking man with a pistol in his hand. They were slowly approaching the house.

Crap. They must have forced The Wiz to talk.

Fallone grabbed the phone and charger, stuffing them in his front pocket. He scrambled up the stairs to the bedroom. When he heard them inside the house, he crawled back onto the roof.

In a flash, he was back on the ground.

As Fallone ran for cover, he could hear the big man bellow.
"FIND HIM!!"

———

Shock Jock wasn't buying it.

Sure, he'd effed up with the underage girls and the coke. Big time. But give his Benjamins to some evangelical head case?

He'd need money, lots of it, to continue greasing his rap star lifestyle. And, of course, pay his mounting legal bills. Besides, he'd never been really comfortable around devout White people. Their faith frightened him.

"Yo B&B, that's messed up," Shock Jock told Bridget and Barry.

They'd convinced Caprice to give them a second chance, revealing that three of the island's wealthiest inhabitants were, in fact, their clients. They were certain they could convince them to donate substantially to the fund, if they could meet with them in person.

So here they were, working their magic on a 6-foot-6 Black man, with neon green hair, tattoo sleeves and a plethora of piercings. They'd rescued Treyon Jones four years ago, when he was forced out of the NBA in disgrace after betting on games – the ones he was about to play in.

Bridget and Barry got the league to agree not to press charges in exchange for a 10-year ban. While technically that meant Jones could apply for reinstatement at the age of 35 – with possibly one or two more years of basketball left in him – he went off and became a rapper instead.

His brush with the law gave him the street cred he needed, because Jones was raised in a suburban, middle-class neighborhood in

Sacramento and didn't know a thing about gangs and guns.

Changing his name, he became a surprise success, with two songs off his debut album CRUSHIN' IT making the charts. Several international tours and records later, Shock Jock was a wealthy man. He had a dozen cars, a private plane, all the sexy women he could handle, and a mansion on Turner Island with a dock for his yacht.

All of it crashed down around him with a sudden fury after the 16-year-old girls went to the police, accompanied by their outraged parents. When the allegations gained traction and the press got wind of it, Shock Jock had little choice.

He called in the fixers.

Barry and Bridget were on the cusp of working out another sweet deal, when the island got overrun by crazy church people. Now they were sitting in front of their client saying they had a deal for that, too.

"Damn girl, I hear you," Shock Jock told Bridget. "I jus' don't believe it. Twenty mil?"

"Consider it a one-time buyout," she said. "Pay the reverend the money and he'll leave you alone. The standoff will end, and we can get back to where we were before: Keeping you out of prison."

"It's a shake-down!"

"Yes, it is," Barry agreed. "But you'll be able to keep the mansion and most of your money. Your music brings in roughly $5 million a year, with live performances. You'll recover in four years."

Shock Jock nodded. The math made sense – if he could stay out of prison. He scanned his temporary quarters – a lounge used by workers at the island's gourmet coffee shop – and scowled.

"Yo B&B, get me outta this dump."

Bridget flashed a dazzling smile.

"Soon as you make the transfer," she said.

CHAPTER

TWENTY

AS THE LADIES sipped their tea and nibbled on cucumber and smoked salmon sandwiches, it occurred to Weathers that under normal circumstances this would be a pleasant diversion.

Margaret Simpson was the island's resident tea maker. She took the art of creating delicious and rather exotic blends very seriously. For this afternoon's gathering, she presented her seasonal mix of Mao Feng and Jasmine Silver Tip green teas, with cardamom, ginger, rose, osmanthus flower and nectarine.

"One of my favorite summer tastes," Simpson said, inhaling the steam rising from her china cup. "Bright, floral and fruity."

"I agree," intoned Natalia Deffontaines. "And you, Cicely?"

"Oh yes," Weathers said. "I can taste the nectarine. So delicious."

"You have a sophisticated palate, my dear," the host said with an appreciative nod.

The small talk and pleasantries continued for a while, but there was no pretending that the men in black standing outside the tea shop's glass front door weren't there. Or that the entire island wasn't under the control of a radical priest and his followers, all of whom

151

despised the rich and privileged.

People like themselves.

Weathers had arranged the get-together with Caprice's consent in order to make her case that the wealthiest islanders should consider contributing to the anti-poverty fund.

The other ladies were sprightly widows in their 70s. They rattled around in the mansions crowning their grand estates, filling their social calendars with dinner parties, shopping excursions and chauffeured outings to the symphony, opera and an occasional play.

Deffontaines' husband had been a highly successful tech entrepreneur with 22 patents to his name, while the tea maker's wealth stemmed from one of the nation's largest chains of big box home improvement stores, founded by Sidney Simpson in 1967.

They each contributed to various charities. They just didn't address the problems facing humanity.

When Weathers broached the subject, as carefully as she could, Deffontaines seemed taken aback.

She was passionate about elephants and had given several million dollars to the World Wildlife Fund on the giant creatures' behalf. She also donated to nonprofits caring for greyhounds and pit bulls that had been abused or neglected.

"We all give in our own ways, Cicely," she said. "I prefer to help animals. They're so innocent, aren't they?"

Simpson had poured millions into the island's only playhouse, converting a former dairy into a small but ornate performing arts showcase that would be the envy of many cities. Interrupting a sold-out production of "Mamma Mia," the building was now housing servants who'd been removed from Billionaire's Row during the takeover.

"The three of us have given generously to various causes," Weathers said. "I just came to the realization that I wasn't helping needy people. I was giving to the academy, the opera house, that sort of thing. But the people who are struggling out there, who can't feed their families, don't have a roof over their heads … I guess I didn't care."

"You mustn't blame yourself, dear," Simpson said. "Don't let that mean preacher upset you."

"He's actually made me think. I went to his church a few days ago and it was quite remarkable. His message about economic justice as a continuation of the civil rights movement really resonated."

Weathers revealed the size of her contribution to Caprice's fund, drawing gasps from the other women.

"We all have more money than we know what to do with," she explained, shrugging. "Why not help the poor? The suffering children?"

Deffontaines nodded.

"Perhaps I am a bit too animal-obsessed," she said. "Human babies are important, too."

"Maybe I can broaden my focus," Simpson put in.

Weathers sipped her tea, feeling victorious.

She reached into her bag and pulled out an eight-page printout listing the more than 300 nonprofits on Caprice's wish list so far. It was growing by the day. The reach was now international, with aid earmarked for a dozen impoverished African nations.

"Plenty to pick from, ladies," she said.

———

The Turner Island standoff was only a few days old, but Caprice knew public opinion was at a tipping point.

News accounts were casting the situation in dark terms, with some outlets describing the church and its followers as "terrorists" or part of a "militant cult." While Stone was accurately portraying what was happening on the island, the harsh spin by outside media had to be softened if the message of inequality was to be heard.

The preacher himself had to be re-cast as a sympathetic figure, driven to extreme measures on behalf of the people.

"Do you know what day today is, Langston?" Carprice asked. It was morning. Day 4 of the standoff.

"Saturday?"

Caprice chuckled. "Yes, but more specifically, it's the Fourth of July."

Langston's usual stony façade returned. He'd learned to wait for Father to explain rather than ask questions prematurely.

"And what do people do on the Fourth? They celebrate the birth of this country."

"Yes, Father."

"Would a group of terrorists intent on slaughtering innocent people celebrate the Fourth?"

"No, Father."

"No, dear Langston, they would not – which is exactly why we will rejoice. Every year, the billionaires here shoot fireworks off a barge. It's considered the best and most extravagant show in the city. Families line the waterfront to catch a glimpse. We won't let that tradition falter.

"We'll fill the sky with a rainbow of sparks, glittering silver showers and scarlet waterfalls," Caprice said brightly. "Have some of the faithful make a large banner declaring HAPPY FOURTH! Display it on the beach closest to the city for all to see.

"Tonight, we change the narrative about who we are and what we're doing here."

"Where are we going to get the fireworks?"

"I assume they're already on the island, ordered weeks ago."

Frankie suddenly appeared. The boy seemed to have an uncanny ability to teleport himself.

"I know where they are," he said, as both Langston and the pastor frowned.

"Son, why aren't you at the school with the others?" Caprice inquired.

"It's booooring there. No video games or nothin.'"

Langston rolled his eyes.

"Sorry, Father. He keeps escaping. I'll put him in a more secure room."

The priest laughed. "And stifle our little Houdini? Heaven's no." To Frankie, he said softly, "What do you know about the fireworks?"

"They're in a big ol' shed. I can take you. There's a whole mess of 'em."

Caprice's eyes were aglow. "Langston, have our young friend here show you the way."

"Yes, Father."

"Oh, and please let Stone know of our holiday plans. Maybe he'll include a mention in his next report."

As promised, Frankie led Langston to a large cache of fireworks in an outbuilding on one of the estates. When word spread of the planned festivities, two of the butlers being held at the community theater said they had experience with pyrotechnic displays and volunteered to set them off.

The show went off flawlessly at the usual time. People gathered across the water to see. Local TV news filmed the event.

As purple and gold flowers filled the sky, Caprice smiled.

Terrorist, indeed.

TWENTY-ONE

BEFORE

"TELL ME ABOUT the drinking, Jeremy."

Stone froze. Words – his stock in trade – escaped him. It was a conversation he knew was coming but dreaded just the same.

The truth was awful, and he didn't want to share it with anyone – even his confessor. The priest who'd seen him at his worst.

The cravings were still intense, even though he'd been discharged and was now coming in strictly for one-on-one counseling and his AA support group. He'd cut his hair short and looked like the youngish professional he was in his khakis, navy blazer and open-collar shirt.

He looked a hell of a lot better than he felt. Good enough on the outside to fool people into thinking he was back on track. Good enough to do the newspaper interviews, find the facts he needed, write the stories.

He wanted to tell the preacher about his freak-show, strobe-light nightmares, but he wouldn't know where to start.

"Stay present. Talk to me," Caprice prodded.

Stone nodded and looked away. Like a machine that needs warming up, he willed himself to speak.

"I've always been a drinker. Since I was like 16, doing keggers with the guys in high school, tapping my parents' liquor cabinet when they were out," he said, his voice barely audible.

"At work it became second nature. Journalists hang out in bars, right? I did my best reporting on a stool. Even the most tight-lipped sources would spill after a few drinks. After work, I'd celebrate a big story with a few beers. Hell, my job interview at the Chronicle was at the M&M. My boss was downing straight Jameson at noon. It's baked into the culture, I guess."

"I see. And you felt the drinking was under control at that time?"

"Yeah, I suppose. I didn't really think about it. I mean, there were nights when I had one too many and had to call a cab. Hangovers here and there. But it never interfered with work."

"And outside of work?"

"I actually drank less when I wasn't working, which may sound a little strange. But I'd be out, you know, doing stuff – mountain biking, kayaking, basketball."

"When did the drinking become a problem?"

Here it comes.

"You know the answer to that, Father."

The preacher's brows furrowed. "I want you to say it."

Another pause. Stone shook his head, girded himself. "My wife killed herself and I'm to blame, okay?"

"Do you want to take a break, Jeremy? You look upset."

"No, I want to get this part over with."

"Good. It's important. Keep going."

"Jenny died and my life went into the crapper. I coped as best I could at the time. I began drinking – *drinking more than usual* – as a form of self-medication. I'm not proud of what happened then, the mistakes I made. And I'm not blaming anyone but myself."

Caprice nodded solemnly. "You've accepted the truth that you are a recovering alcoholic and that you will be for the rest of your life. But you still haven't been completely honest with me."

Stone looked puzzled. "What do you mean?"

"You've relapsed, haven't you?"

Jesus, how could he possibly know?

"No."

"Please don't lie to me. If we can't completely trust each other, I can't help you. Do you want to be helped, Jeremy?"

Stone fought back tears. He'd lost control one night, when the pain got too severe and the demons too persuasive. When his designated support group "friend" didn't return his call right away. Drank himself into a stupor at a dive bar and afterward pretended that nothing happened.

"Okay, okay. I got drunk one night. I screwed up. There, you happy?"

It was Caprice's turn to be silent. He stared intensely at Stone for a while.

"That's all for today," the preacher said. "I want you to think about what you're not telling me, what you may have suppressed in your subconscious because it's too terrible to face."

"There's nothing. I'm sharing everything."

"Not everything. Not yet."

"I swear."

Caprice smiled. His golden eyes shined with kindness and understanding.

"Perhaps I'm being too hard on you. It's possible that you don't yet know the full truth," he said. "The blackouts you've experienced can make it difficult to tell fact from fiction, dream state from reality.

Your memories may be sliced into fragments, seemingly unrelated to one another. It's like a jigsaw puzzle in a way. I'm urging you to put the pieces together to get the clearest possible understanding of your past. Does that make sense?"

"Sure, I guess," Stone said. "I'll do my best."

"Thank you, Jeremy. I know you will."

Stone left the clinic in a daze. All that truth-telling. It was like walking over broken glass. And now he was being asked to dig deeper, to another level of hell, in search of what? Puzzle pieces?

When he got to his car, he looked around the parking lot. He saw nothing unusual, but he couldn't shake the feeling.

Am I being followed?

————

Aiden McHenry was a simple man with an extraordinary talent.

He could turn invisible.

That super power came in handy in his line of work, which chiefly involved tailing people without their knowledge – and always without their consent. People hired him because he had an uncanny ability to surveil human targets without ever tipping his hand. In fact, he claimed to have never been detected, a track record he was quite proud of.

That's why Langston paid him a visit one day at his office, a corner stool at a bustling bar. One look at the fridge-sized former cop and McHenry knew Langston couldn't do the job himself. He stood out, in a frightening sort of way.

McHenry, on the other hand, was the Invisible Man. He could be sitting at the bar next to a subject, or playing pool one table over, and he was immediately forgotten. His car, so very ordinary in size and appearance, also seemed to fade into nothingness. He'd mastered the art of disappearing, even while taking notes and snapping incriminating photos.

"Got a job for you," Langston said. "Need you to keep tabs on someone."

"For you or that poor people's church of yours?" McHenry was a simple man, but he insisted on having clients who could pay.

Langston's eyes narrowed. He dropped a fat envelope on the lacquered bar.

McHenry gave the contents a quick approving glance. He opened his black leather bomber jacket and stuffed the wad of cash in an inside pocket.

"You've got my attention," he said. "Who's getting shadowed?"

"A reporter for the Chronicle. Jeremy Stone," Langston said, as quietly as he could. He handed over a photo of Stone. "Just got out of rehab, but he's been relapsing."

McHenry scratched his three-day-old stubble. "And why do you and the reverend care?"

"Father has a special interest in this one. I'll leave it at that. Follow him at night for a few weeks. Let me know where he goes, how much he's boozing, that kind of thing."

"Sure," McHenry said, draining his beer. "Pleasure doing business."

Then he disappeared without anyone noticing.

TWENTY-TWO

DESPITE HIS long hours, Fallone didn't live on the Andrews-Weathers estate. Like most of the island's workers, he shuttled in and out from the city.

He broke the curfew regularly, but Weathers looked the other way, finding his presence at night comforting.

Since the siege began, Fallone had been sneaking into the mansion through an unwatched back door late at night in order to eat and sleep. He was careful to always have a snack for Arrow, who wasn't much of a guard dog but had a shrill bark. He kept the lights off and removed his shoes, preferring to pad around in the dark as silently as possible.

When he finally was able to call McCoy, he whispered.

"Joey, that you?" the detective asked. "Can barely hear you."

"Yeah, it's me. I'm still on the island. Been on the run the past four days. They're chasing me."

"Where are you?"

"At my clients' house. I'm the only one here, but they're patrolling the area. That's why I gotta whisper, pal."

"Sure, gotcha."

"Hey, I've been out doing some recon. I can pass along some info about their manpower, defenses, that sort of thing."

"That'll help. But first there's something I need to tell you."

"Sure, what's up?"

"The school and other buildings may be rigged to blow. The barricade, too. I saw crates of explosives in one of those trucks you warned me about."

"Damn." Fallone shook his head. Cicely was in more danger than he'd thought.

"Have you seen anything?"

"Nah, but, hey, I haven't been looking for bombs."

"Can you? I don't want to put you even more in harm's way, but SWAT and the National Guard are preparing to go in as soon as tomorrow, tanks and all. If explosives are detonated at that school, with all those people, we could have a friggin' massacre."

"I was there the other day. There's a sentry at the door and another making the rounds, but I can take a closer look."

"Please hurry. The clock is counting down, buddy."

"Okay, man. I'll text you what I know so far, then head straight over there."

"That's great. I'll tell the chief."

"Hey, Mike, what's this all about? Taking over the island."

McCoy took a deep breath. "Hell if I know. Preacher and his clones are demanding 'economic justice.' It's all BS."

"Yeah," Fallone said, although part of him admired the audacity of it all. "Call you again when it's safe."

Minutes later, he sent a detailed message that included the number and rough locations of the roaming patrols he'd encountered, how many men were watching the school and barricade, and where some of the key people were being housed, including Stone and Sterling, but not Caprice or Weathers. He added information about disabled boats and helicopters, and noted that there seemed to be a conspicuous absence of guns and other weapons.

Everyone appeared to be reporting to Caprice and his lieutenant, he concluded.

As he was preparing to slip out for some more recon, a key turned in the front door.

Fallone ducked behind a wall seconds before Weathers stepped inside. Amazingly, she was alone.

As she was taking off her coat, the security man crept up behind her. He put his hand over her mouth.

"Don't scream, it's me," he said in a low voice.

After a moment, he removed his hand. Weathers, suddenly overcome with emotion, began to cry. He helped her to a sofa and held her close.

"I'm glad you're alright," he said. "I spent the past few days combing the island, looking for you."

"I'm fine. I was so worried about *you*, though. When nobody knew where you were, I got scared."

"What are you doing here? Back home, I mean."

Wiping away tears, Weathers shrugged. "The reverend's orders. Anyone who contributes to the fund and is sincere about it is being allowed to go home."

Fallone wondered what constituted sincerity in the mind of a radical priest. And under the circumstances, could any donation be truly considered voluntary?

"I'd like to stay and talk, but I have to go," he told her. "A cop I know on the outside told me that Caprice's men may have explosives.

I need to check around the school."

"Oh my God! There are more than a hundred people being held there."

"Would Caprice do something like that?" Fallone said, zipping up his gray hoodie.

"I don't think so," she said. "But I wouldn't have thought he'd lead an attack on Turner Island either."

Fallone nodded and headed for the door.

"What will they do to you if they catch you?" Weathers called out, but he was already gone.

———

All this talk of explosives unnerved the mayor.

It was one thing to send in the army and police. They had the zealots outmanned roughly 20 to one. They had enough tanks, copters and boats to hit every part of the little island simultaneously.

But Pucci couldn't shake his fears.

If the school and community theater really were booby-trapped, scores of innocent people could be killed. If the tanks rolled and bombs went off, the blood would be on his hands.

Quite simply, his political career would be over. Nobody would cast a vote for the mayor who caused a slaughter.

"I've got my dick in a ringer, Upps," he told his adviser privately. "Where the hell is this secret source of ours? Are there effing bombs or not?"

Upps was gazing out the window. "You heard the chief at the briefing, Sal. Their man Fallone is checking the school as we speak."

"Why's it taking so long?"

"Relax. He can't simply stroll over there and look around, now can he? Try to be patient."

Pucci got up to pour himself a stiff drink. Before he could taste a drop, though, his phone rang. He didn't recognize the number but assumed correctly that it was Caprice.

The mayor put the call on speaker and waved over Upps.

"Hello, reverend."

"Mr. Mayor. I'm calling to arrange something, if you're willing."

"Go on."

"Meet me in person. Just you and me, here on the island. I give you my word that you won't be harmed or detained in any way."

"And why would I take that risk, when we can talk like we are now, on the phone?"

"Because I need to look you in the eyes. And because I suspect you don't want the blood of innocent people staining your legacy. A negotiated end to the world's most-watched standoff, on the other hand, would make you a shoo-in for another term."

That made a lot of sense, Pucci had to admit. If he could get safely past the whole bomb thing. He looked across his desk, saw Upps giving him a thumb's up.

"Okay, let's talk," the mayor said.

"Tomorrow at noon. Bring no one."

———

Langston had a problem. One of the security men, it turned out, had eluded capture.

Worse, he was crisscrossing the island, recruiting allies and likely communicating with police on the mainland.

Still, every problem has its solution. It's just a question of finding it. That's what Father had taught him during their counseling, when he pulled himself out of his haze and found God.

The security man named Fallone had slipped through their fingers more than once, but now they had him at last. Following Weathers back to her home was a good idea. If everything went well in the next few minutes, he'd have Father to thank for that.

Langston adjusted his night vision binoculars and allowed himself a tight grin.

Fallone, the hood of his sweatshirt concealing his face, was on the move. He resembled a Ninja the way he slipped through the trees, making his way down the boulevard.

"He'll be heading for the school," he told one of the men in black. "Let's take him there. Alert the others."

The man hustled off, leaving Langston alone with his thoughts.

For every problem, there's a solution.

TWENTY-THREE

SALVATORE ALBERTO Pucci was not a brave man.

He relied on cunning not brawn, which was important for a man who stood just 5-foot-4 – a height unchanged since grade school. It was smarts that allowed him to best bullies growing up, figuring out their weaknesses and insecurities, and applying the right amount of pressure.

The same proved true in the brutal world of politics, with its mudslinging and festering lies. Find the weakness in your opponent and release the hounds. Tear the bastard apart. That was his mantra and it worked very well.

It didn't matter if the dirt you were spreading was true or not, Pucci knew. It just had to take root in the minds of enough voters to sway an election.

As he walked slowly across the bridge's no-man's land, between the cops and the zealots, Pucci steadied himself by doing what he did best: plotting. He'd taken down many adversaries in the past. Found their pressure points.

When it came to the radical priest, Pucci thought he held the strings, had a way to keep him in line with those millions in city contracts. He attended the occasional service at People's Oasis, pretended to be supportive, merely to placate a man who posed a growing threat. What was that line about holding enemies close?

But with his bodacious plot to seize an island filled with rich people, Caprice had turned the tables.

How could anyone control someone so willing to go to prison for a cause? As the mayor anxiously approached the barricade, he decided to play the one card up his sleeve.

He'd offer Caprice a deal.

One virtually impossible to resist.

———

That's odd, Fallone thought.

The usual sentry positioned at the school entrance was gone. There were no obvious patrols either.

It would be easy for him to check for explosives. Almost too easy.

Something was off. The church had to be closely watching the people being held hostage inside, their human poker chips. So, where the heck were they?

From behind a tree, Fallone scanned the nearby storefronts and rooftops but saw nothing out of the ordinary. Maybe it was his lucky day. Maybe it was a trap. *What to do?*

He bit his lip, trying to focus. McCoy and the others were counting on him. Cicely, too.

Emerging from his leafy cover, he ran in a half-crouch to the stone wall that formed the edge of the school property. Looking for signs of charges or detonation wires, he made his way to the entrance.

Looking all around the massive door, painted red with a curved top, he found nothing. He continued down the wall on the other side. Still nothing.

Looks like a false alarm.

He was about to call McCoy from another hiding place when he heard a twig snap.

Fallone looked up and saw a huge man eyeing him with a sinister glare. He had a gun in his hand.

"Mr. Fallone," Langston said. "We meet again."

———

Caprice had nothing to offer the mayor, nor was he in the mood to bargain.

He was merely stalling.

Contributions had started flowing into the fund, which now totaled more than $100 million. He'd been wise to give Bridget and Barry another chance to prove their worth – once he provided the proper motivation, of course.

They'd gotten all of their deeply flawed clients to contribute, including an abusive rapper and two wealthy businessmen accused in federal indictments of financial crimes and coverups.

But it was Weathers who proved to be the most useful.

When she attended his sermon a few days before the takeover, he could tell just by looking in her eyes. She *believed*. And once that Rubicon had been crossed, once the doubts and pessimism disappear, believers were invaluable.

The note she wrote was merely a confirmation of what he already knew: If properly utilized, Weathers could be the catalyst he needed to kickstart his anti-poverty initiative, gently persuading her wealthy neighbors to climb aboard.

The fact that they were under duress while making their donations didn't bother the pastor. Not at all. The important thing was to alter their thinking about the underclass. And if it took the invasion of Turner Island to accomplish that, so be it.

It was unfortunate that he had to have Langston follow Weathers, put her home under surveillance, but there was a man on the loose – a dangerous man. He had to be controlled.

So far, not a soul had been seriously injured. That was something Caprice could use to his advantage, but hardly a hard-and-fast part of the plan. Never in the history of the world had there been a revolution that didn't require sacrifice. There had always been a price, paid in blood. Often, buckets and buckets of it.

He saw the rotund mayor coming his way, escorted by Langston. They looked so odd together, like total opposites. One sweaty and round, the other cool and built like a walking mountain.

They were meeting in the small park where Caprice often meditated on a stone bench, framed by fragrant, pink-petaled peonies.

The pastor didn't rise to greet Pucci. Instead, he waved for the mayor to sit next to him.

"Thanks for meeting me," Caprice said.

Pucci dotted his forehead with a handkerchief. He looked haggard, like he hadn't slept in days, which was pretty much true.

"I only wish it was under better circumstances," the mayor said. "You have a lot of people worried, myself included."

"Of course. If you weren't worried, there would be something wrong with you. But I can assure you that nobody on the island has been harmed."

"That detective you held didn't look very good."

"Well, I did say *on the island*. We released him, after all."

Pucci frowned. "Excuse me for getting straight to the point, but you need to know something. This standoff of yours has to end immediately. The governor wants the National Guard to move in as early as tomorrow morning, and I do not intend to stand in the way any longer."

"I see."

"You've accomplished what you set out to do. You've delivered your message. You've raised money for the poor. Hell, you've shamed some of the world's richest people into doing your bidding. Congratulations. But it's over now. Time's up."

"Not according to God," Caprice said pleasantly. "And whose commands matter most: The Lord Almighty or hizzoner?"

"Have you lost all touch with reality, reverend? You're willing to sacrifice innocent people because of some kind of twisted vision?"

"I can see why you think it's twisted – or a threat. King was leading a revolution, giving power to the have-nots. Navalny, too. And we know what happened to them."

"So, you want to be a martyr, is that it? And you refuse to leave?"

Caprice laughed. "Hardly. As I said before, I intend to leave this place peacefully, when the time comes."

"Right. So you've said."

Frustrated, the mayor played his only card.

"Look, nobody has been killed. Surrender today and I will recommend leniency: Probation, no prison time. You can keep every cent in that fund, minus any expenses for property damage, as long as the contributions weren't coerced."

Caprice seemed genuinely surprised. It really was a sweet offer. He tugged his beard and thought for a few moments.

"And the others? The men and women who believe in the cause

and followed me here?"

"Same. Probation and restitution."

"Let me talk to them," the priest said after reflecting for a few moments. "I'll give you an answer in two hours."

TWENTY-FOUR

TALKING TO THE imprisoned islanders, getting documents personally selected by Caprice – it wasn't enough.

Stone could see what was happening with his own eyes, of course, but even that could be manipulated. A mirage shimmering in the desert.

No, it wasn't nearly enough. In order to find the truth and inform the world, he needed proof – much more than he'd been spoon-fed so far.

Under the guise of looking for people to interview, Stone began searching for the location of the computers that the church had to be using to develop its donation-worthy list of nonprofits and facilitate bank transfers.

He'd spent the past two days zig-zagging through The Commons and surrounding businesses until he crossed every non-residential building off his list. The church had to be set up in one of the vacated homes, but which one? How could he possibly know?

Stone shook his head in frustration. His search seemed futile. But then it occurred to him that Caprice would savor the irony of pumping up his fund in the unlikeliest of places: Sterling's opulent mansion.

At a brisk pace, he headed toward Billionaire's Row, then suddenly stopped, realizing that he couldn't waltz inside the computer room and start browsing. With millions of dollars flowing in and out, it'd likely be guarded. He'd have to find a way to get inside undetected. Sneak a peek. With any luck, learn what was going on through hard evidence, not handouts.

To do that, he'd first need to lose his shadow.

Trailing about 20 paces, his chaperone was a fit, wiry man in his 20s wearing a black track suit and sneakers. Stone doubted he could outrun him.

The reporter pondered the situation for a moment, then changed direction, veering sharply to his left. He smiled at the escort and waved his notebook, then entered the private school once more.

He found Frankie playing on his cot with a model airplane. Some kind of fighter jet in gray plastic. The boy was making loud "zoom-zoom" sounds.

"Hey kid," Stone whispered, moving close. "You know how to slip outta here, right?"

Frankie immediately brightened. "Heck yeah. Do it all the time."

"Great. See that man over there?"

Still holding the toy plane, Frankie nodded. Stone's personal watchman was leaning casually against a wall, out of earshot but maintaining eye contact.

"I need to shake him. Can you help me?"

"Sure thing, mister. There's a ceiling vent in the bathroom that I've been using." Flashing a mischievous grin, he pulled a handful of screws from his pants pocket. "Stand on the toilet. Leads outside."

The boy gave Stone an appraising glance. "You should fit."

"Follow me to the can," the reporter said. "When the man comes, tell him I'm sick. That should buy me enough time."

Minutes later, Stone was pulling himself up into the ventilation shaft as Frankie stood watch outside. As predicted, the escort soon appeared.

"I wouldn't go in there," the boy told him, wrinkling his nose.

"Oh yeah, why's that?"

"He's been puking. Real nasty."

The man put his ear to the door. Hearing nothing, he looked back at Frankie, who shrugged and made more "zoom" sounds.

The man, frowning, went inside. Seeing no one, he began searching the stalls.

They were all empty.

———

Stone's hunch was right.

Grateful for the lack of the usual security detail, he wound his way around the massive home, peering into windows. When he made it to the rear garden, scaling a decorative wrought-iron fence, he hit the jackpot.

A man and a woman were seated at a table, the light from the screens of laptops giving their faces an eerie glow. As Stone crept closer, he heard the woman's cellphone buzz.

She said something to the man that made him laugh, then picked up her satchel and left. Minutes passed before the man got up, yawned and stretched his arms over his head. He put a cigarette between his lips and disappeared.

Here's my chance.

As quietly as he could, Stone twisted the knob on the patio door and entered the room. The man had left his laptop on, revealing a spreadsheet packed with nonprofits. Dozens and dozens of them, with notes on their missions, budgets, number of employees and funding status.

Stone scrolled down, seeing that many of the groups had apparently been wired funds ranging from a low of $500,000 to a whopping $25 million.

"It's really happening," Stone muttered. "I'll be damned."

Scattered around the table were papers listing eligible organizations, not only in the United States but around the world.

Pawing through them, Stone saw the names of Weathers and other wealthy donors scrawled in the margins. He was about to pocket the most detailed list, when he heard a noise.

He popped to his feet, but it was too late.

Stone turned to see Caprice looking at him quizzically.

"Always digging," the priest said with a sprinkle of admiration. "Never satisfied."

"That's true," Stone said, gathering himself. "Besides, you would have said no."

"I merely wanted you to be patient. All would have been revealed in short order. But I suppose I was asking too much." Caprice took a deep breath. "Well, *c'est la vie*. Do you believe me now, Jeremy?"

Stone nodded, feeling a tad flustered after being caught in the act.

"I had to see for myself," he said. "You get that, right? I can't just take you at your word."

The printout was still in Stone's right hand, neatly folded in half. Caprice eyed it suspiciously.

"What were you going to do with that?"

"I don't know. Maybe talk to a few more donors. Include some of the facts in my next report."

"Then take it."

"Thanks."

The man who'd left his laptop on returned from his smoke break. He looked even more embarrassed than Stone, but Caprice's gaze was locked on his chosen journalist.

"Jeremy?"

"Yeah?"

"Try asking next time. I may surprise you."

TWENTY-FIVE

ONE BY ONE, the richest men and women on the island were returning to their lush homes.

Stone interviewed many of them, and they all said the same thing: They'd donated willingly to Caprice's fund. After some reflection – and listening to Weathers, whom most respected – they decided it was the right thing to do.

Over and over, they stressed that nobody forced them to wire the bank. Nobody put a gun to their heads.

It was a real head-scratcher. Stone was far too cynical to accept such a miraculous group conversion, but how could he ignore the facts? The anti-poverty fund had swollen to an impressive $250 million.

"It's happening, Jeremy," Caprice said, looking somewhat amazed by his own success. "We've compiled a comprehensive list of worthy nonprofits here and abroad, and we're already starting to distribute funds. It's … the greatest thrill of my life."

Caprice had set a stunning goal of $1 billion, but the richest man on Turner Island – the one who could instantly make that target a reality – was still holding out. Sterling even turned away Weathers, whom he accused of being "brainwashed."

All of that was in Stone's notes as he faced the camera yet again.

"This is Jeremy Stone. As the standoff here marks a sixth day, there are major developments.

"Reverend Caprice, the leader of the radical group holding the island, met today with Mayor Salvatore Pucci in hopes of negotiating an end to the siege. Caprice will be addressing his followers this evening.

"The mayor is threatening to re-take the island militarily as soon as tomorrow morning if Caprice doesn't surrender, according to the priest and his followers. It isn't immediately clear whether Pucci made the church leader any sort of offer in exchange for his cooperation.

"The people being held at the private school here are being treated well, from what I've been able to see. Some of the wealthiest residents have been returning to their homes on so-called Billionaire's Row.

"The anti-poverty fund established by the church has received more than a quarter-billion dollars in donations. I've seen evidence of that and talked to several of the billionaires who live on the island. They state unequivocally that their contributions were not coerced in any way. Hugo Sterling, the owner of Galactix, remains the single biggest holdout.

"Meanwhile, people being detained here are fearful as to what may happen next."

Stone went on to recap his interviews with several of the detainees, including Cavill, who had proven to be one of the most quotable.

"Will Caprice and his followers surrender? Will authorities invade? We should have answers very soon. This is Jeremy Stone, reporting from Turner Island."

Caprice, as always, was in the wings listening intently.

"Nicely done," the pastor said when the live feed ended. "I respect the way you refuse to speculate, reporting just the facts."

"That's the only way I know how. It doesn't bother you that I said people here are afraid?"

"That's the truth. We'd be foolish not to be."

"Suppose so," Stone said, shoving the notebook back in his pocket. "When the soldiers and tanks come, it won't be pretty."

Caprice grew silent for a few moments, then stuck out a closed hand.

"A gift for you, Jeremy."

He opened his fingers, revealing Stone's black cellphone. Astonished, the reporter hesitated briefly before grabbing the sleek device.

"What's this? You suddenly trust me now?"

Caprice sighed. "I've always had enormous faith in you. This just means we're getting near the end."

"No more restrictions? No more escorts and time limits?"

"None."

Stone eyed the priest suspiciously.

"And I can still leave any time I want?"

"Of course," Caprice said. "But you'll want to see this story through to the end. The final chapters are about to unfold."

———

The first person Stone called was Betters.

He could hear her choking up as he assured her that he was safe and hadn't been harmed. He described the thick tension covering the island like a fog as the standoff neared its conclusion.

"What have they kept you from reporting?" she asked.

"They restricted who I could talk to at first. Also, the information about the fund. I wasn't able to do any digging, confirm the things they were saying. Plus, everywhere I went, I was being watched."

"You're putting that in past tense."

"That's right. Caprice just gave my phone back, promised me total freedom. Guess I'll be putting that to the test."

Betters laughed. "I figured you'd want to stay, no matter the risk. You've never walked away from a promising exposé."

"Yeah, that's true. I am scared, though. I'd hate to go down in a hail of bullets fired by a nervous National Guardsman."

"You'll be fine. Just keep your head down," Betters said, only to immediately regret the advice.

The editor had seen the footage of tanks and other war machines rumbling through the city on their way to the bridge. Nervous Guardsmen would be the least of Stone's worries.

Changing the subject, she brought up the whole TV stardom thing.

"Your fan mail is pouring in," she said. "From all over the world. You're apparently huge in Japan. A toy company there is making an action figure."

"Good Lord."

"And, brace yourself, you've got competing book deal offers. HarperCollins, Simon & Schuster … Sony wants to buy the movie rights. If you survive to tell the tale, you'll be both famous and rich."

"How do you know all this?"

"The Chronicle has become all things Jeremy Stone," Betters said, her usual sarcastic tone returning. "We had to hire two staffers just to handle the flood of email and phone calls."

"How's ol' Burgess doing? Freaking out?"

"Oh no, he's loving every minute of it. Absolutely certain we're getting a Pulitzer. We run every word you say on the air in the paper, in case you didn't know. Your signoff has become a meme."

"I'm sick of it, to tell the truth. Can't wait to start writing for the paper again."

"I'll take it," Betters said. "You sound good. Keeping the booze at bay?"

That was an interesting way to put it. Every time he passed the door under the stairs, he still heard the bottles calling his name.

"Yeah, I'm okay. Serious and sober. Look, I better let you get back to work. If I survive tomorrow, I'll file a goddamn story."

"Be careful, Jeremy," she said. "I can't believe I'm saying this, but I actually miss your sorry White ass."

TWENTY-SIX

END POVERTY NOW was the sort of essential nonprofit that rarely grabs headlines.

The coalition stocked the food banks that kept low-income families from starving, operated a clinic and mobile medical service that served rural communities and migrant farm workers, and provided tenants facing eviction and other threats with free legal services.

It was the kind of low-key lifeboat work that never ended and was never enough. Volunteers came and went, citing both heartbreak and burnout.

And, so it was, on a typical morning – with parents lining up for several blocks for the first crack at government surplus milk, cheese and baby formula – that Tracy O'Connor burst out laughing.

The executive director was pointing at the computer screen in her cluttered basement office. The organization's bank account was showing a deposit of $10 million – more than a dozen times bigger than the entire annual operating budget. It was like the Monopoly game card: *Bank error in your favor.*

Other staffers circled behind her. Soon, the room was echoing with gales of laughter. Anyone passing by at that moment would have thought they'd all gone crazy.

"Thank you very much, Bank of America. Much appreciated," O'Connor said, triggering more guffaws.

From a corner of the room, a volunteer shouted over the din.

"Guys! Check out this email that just came in."

O'Connor called it up. She read the message out loud.

"To the Unsung Heroes," it began. "Your tireless work hasn't gone unnoticed. To bolster your efforts now and in the future, please accept the $10 million donation that has been wired to your account. There are no strings attached. We trust you will spend the money wisely. Sincerely, People's Oasis Church."

This can't be real, O'Connor thought.

So many times, she'd fought for scraps of state, federal and foundation grants, staying up late night after night to write detailed proposals only to be disappointed. And suddenly, out of nowhere, millions of dollars come unsolicited?

"That's the church that's taken over the island with all the rich people!" the volunteer exclaimed. "I read that they set up some kind of fund to help the poor, got billionaires to chip in."

Excited murmurs swept the room like an electrical current.

"That's right," O'Connor said as she Googled the church. She stabbed at a recent picture of Caprice, smiling like a modern-day Jesus. "It's this guy. He's been preaching about lifting up the have-nots. His sermons are all over YouTube."

"So, the money in our account – it's legit?" someone asked.

"I think so. Let's treat it like any other donation," the director said, rising to her feet. She wiped away tears of joy. "I'm going to notify the board of directors. Let's give them a list of projects and programs.

Everything we've wanted to do for the community, but couldn't."

People began hugging one another. Some danced to imaginary music.

"Think big!" O'Connor implored.

Within hours, the horde of reporters covering the standoff got wind of the money flowing out of Turner Island into the coffers of chronically underfunded grassroots groups.

The beneficiaries were all nonprofits – addressing poverty, hunger, homelessness, addiction, access to health care and a host of other pressing issues – in seemingly every part of the nation.

RADICAL PRIEST BECOMES ROBIN HOOD blared one newspaper headline. NONPROFITS STUNNED BY MEGA DONATIONS read another.

By sunrise on the sixth day of the standoff, Caprice was being hailed in the media as a hero and, quite possibly, a future saint.

It was a stunning turn of events, given how the takeover was initially portrayed as a violent attack and Caprice as a sinister cult leader.

Leaders of charitable organizations were now taking turns praising the reverend, some tearfully.

"He's done more to help the poor and afflicted in the past week than we've accomplished in this country in 20 years," O'Connor said in a TV interview. "I just hope I can shake his hand one day."

———

While police officials suspected there might be as many as a hundred religious zealots holding the island, in truth there were only 24.

Seventeen men and seven women.

With the exception of a pair who stood watch over the school and two more remaining at the barricade, they all gathered at the park on a moonless night to listen to their leader.

Caprice didn't use a microphone. He merely stood and faced them, causing an immediate hush.

"Good evening. Are we feeling the power of the Lord?"

"Yes, Father!"

"Are we doing His holy work?"

"Yes, Father!"

"I'm glad, because what we are doing here is not for the faint of heart," he said. "What we are doing is for the brave and the determined. Revolutions require such grit, my friends. And that's exactly what this is: a revolution. Every day, we are opening more hearts and minds.

"Every day, our message spreads further and further, to the far corners of the globe. And it's not just the poor who are being uplifted, but the richest of the rich as well. They were blind, but now they see. They finally see what we've been preaching about all these years. They've finally opened both their hearts and their vaults. And all we're seeking is a small piece of that treasure.

"I've asked you to come here tonight because I have something important to tell you. The mayor has notified me that in the morning he will give the command to respond to the occupation with military force – unless we all surrender immediately. He has promised that none of us will be imprisoned for our actions if we do what he asks."

A chorus of boos rose up from the crowd.

Caprice put out his hands and the clamor ceased.

"Please listen carefully. I am your spiritual leader, yes, but I will not decide something so important for you. You must reach your own decision. If you stay, you will certainly be arrested. You may even be killed. If you leave, well, you have the mayor's pledge.

"So, I want all of you to kneel and pray silently for the next 60 seconds. Then I will ask for your decision."

Everyone, including Caprice, took a knee. The only sound was the chirping of crickets.

When the priest rose, his disciples did the same. He examined their earnest faces and knew, but he posed the question anyway.

"Anyone who wishes to leave, raise your hand," he called out.

Nobody moved.

"Those who wish to carry on …"

A sea of hands shot up before the priest could finish. People shouted and jumped in jubilation. Then they began to chant.

FA-THER!

FA-THER!

———

Fallone wondered why Caprice's bodyguard was toying with him.

He could have put a bullet in his brain. Crushed his skull with a couple of blows from those Hulk-like hammer fists.

Instead, he was playing games. Skirting the big question.

They'd stuffed him in a windowless underground room with only a chair and a cot. Two men were standing by the only door.

"You suck as an interrogator," Fallone said with a sneer.

"That so?"

"Yeah, you haven't even asked what I was doing out there."

"I *know* what you were doing."

"So, are there bombs or not?"

"I might as well tell you, since they'll be attacking in the morning,"

Langston said with a slit of a grin. "There are no explosives. Those were dummy crates your friend saw. We stenciled on the markings, really for the drones to see, but McCoy did us a favor, telling everyone on the mainland that we were preparing for Armageddon."

He formed a mushroom cloud with his huge hands. "*Boom!*"

"Why? Why would you pretend?"

"It bought us a few days, didn't it? Had you on your hands and knees. Flushed you out of your hiding place. And got us this."

He showed the borrowed phone that Fallone had risked his life for.

"We sent your pal a text, telling him the school was wired. Hopefully, it'll give us a bit more time, but it doesn't really matter. Our work here is nearly done."

"What work is that? Terrorizing people? Forcing them to do your bidding? What a great, humanitarian church you belong to."

Langston stared at the prisoner in a frightening way but said nothing.

"What are you going to do with me?" asked Fallone, suddenly unnerved.

"Don't worry. Father doesn't want you hurt. I'm going to release you, in fact. At the barricade, when the tanks come."

"No thanks, I'm fine here."

The enforcer chortled. It sounded like a car backfiring.

"You're just another non-believer," he said. "You deserve what's coming to you. You all do."

He stomped out of the room. The heavy door clanged shut with a thunderous echo. A deadbolt slid into place.

Fallone cursed. For the first time since the island was overrun, there was nothing he could do.

———

The mayor wasn't having a good evening.

The first blow was the call from Caprice informing him that, "after careful consideration and prayerful reflection," he and his flock had decided not to surrender until their work was completed. That was followed about an hour later by news that the source on the island had confirmed that explosives were indeed ringing the school.

After receiving the alarming text from Fallone, McCoy immediately notified the chief. It was curious that Fallone didn't send along any photos of the bombs, but the detective attributed that to his friend's reluctance to linger at guarded locations.

Fallone would call when it was safe, McCoy thought.

Pucci, meanwhile, felt he had no choice.

After consulting with his most trusted advisers, he ordered police and the National Guard to stand down. He had his aides prepare for a morning press conference.

"Given this new information, we can't go in with force," the mayor told Winterbrook over the phone. "There are simply too many lives at stake."

TWENTY-SEVEN

THERE WERE WHIRLWIND romances, and then there's what transpired in one frenzied weekend between Ashley Lynn Summers and Hugo Sterling.

It started on a Friday night in a theater off the Vegas strip, where Summers was one of the featured showgirls in a retro stage production, complete with a live band and Elvis and Sinatra impersonators.

She wore a rhinestone-encrusted silver bra, g-string bottom and towering headdress adorned with snowy ostrich feathers that was billed as "glamorous."

She'd given notice before the show that this was her final performance, having scored a modeling gig involving French lingerie that had the potential, according to her manager, to propel her into ads on social media.

From his VIP table, Sterling saw Summers come on stage, all shiny and leggy, and was immediately entranced. When she smiled and locked arms with the other girls for their high kicks, the twice-divorced billionaire knew he had to meet her.

He'd just ended a relationship with a former Vogue cover girl who had a budding career as an actress after notching critically acclaimed supporting roles in several indie films. Sterling found her to be too independent for his taste. Her insistence on visiting her highly educated New England family every month was another turn-off. *But this showgirl.* She could be the one to devote herself absolutely to him. He had a gut feeling, and his gut was seldom wrong.

With hundred-dollar bills, Sterling greased his way backstage. He was standing nervously outside the dressing room when she appeared. Her top was off, along with the feathers. She saw him and yawned.

"Sorry, been on my feet all day. I'm sore all over," she said, bending over to massage her shapely calves. "Arnie says you wanted to see me?"

He did his level best not to stare.

"I'm Hugo Sterling. I own a hotel here, among other things. There's a hot tub and champagne in the penthouse suite. Also, a masseuse on call. Would do wonders for those legs."

She straightened and studied him for a minute. "Are you asking me out, like on a date?"

"Yeah, guess I am."

"You rich or something?"

He laughed. "I'm so rich I don't know how to spend it all. I can use some help."

"Is that right." She frowned and belatedly covered her breasts with an arm. "Well, I'm not a prostitute, if that's what you're thinking. I don't screw around for money."

"Of course not. You're far too beautiful for that."

"What hotel?"

"Excuse me?"

"What hotel is yours?"

"Oh, Galactix, down from Bellagio."

"The one shaped like a spaceship?"

"That's right."

She called for Arnie, the stage manager, who quickly jogged over. "Does this man … *what's your name again?*"

"Hugo Sterling."

"Does Hugo Sterling own Galactix on The Strip?"

Arnie, who had one of Sterling's hundreds in his wallet, nodded extravagantly. "He sure does."

"Told you," Sterling said with a wink as Arnie disappeared, becoming part of the post-show commotion.

Summers looked impressed.

While it was admittedly superficial to be attracted to someone because of their money, she couldn't help herself. She was 26 and rooming with two of the girls from the show, with a balance of $1,450 in her checking account and an aging Fiat in dire need of a valve job.

Sterling looked to be approaching 60 and a bit flabby, but she was willing to overlook that. Having grown up in a trailer park with three brothers and an alcoholic mother, all scraping by on government assistance, she craved security, something the man in front of her could provide in spades. As Tina Turner famously sang, what's love got to do with it?

"I'm Ashley," she said with a radiant smile. "Give me five minutes to change."

He proposed two days later, apologizing for the mere 28-carat diamond on her ring. They married just a week after that – not in some trashy Vegas chapel, but while orbiting the Earth on a Galactix shuttle. They exchanged vows floating in zero gravity. The prenup treated her generously.

In the years that followed, Sterling jetted her to the finest resorts around the world, surprised her with a silver Bugatti Chiron with SHWGRL plates and showered her with jewelry. He even allowed her to choose the new yacht and redecorate the home on Turner Island.

The extravagant gifts were nice, but after a while she wished he'd stop.

It felt like he was trying to buy her affection and that part of her wasn't for sale.

———

Caprice had been a decent marriage counselor as a priest, not a great one.

How could he be, when he lacked first-hand knowledge of intimate relationships? Still, he had an inexhaustible supply of empathy and was a good listener, both of which were essential attributes for the dispensing of advice.

What he was about to do, though, cut against the grain. He was headed to Ashley Sterling's quarters with information that would likely damage – not build – trust in her marriage.

The priest knocked on the door and smiled when she appeared in a pink satin robe. Rushed out of her mansion without any makeup, she looked strangely pallid. Hair spilled over her forehead in unbrushed rivulets.

"Sorry to disturb you," he said. "May I come in?"

They sat together in the dining room of the vacant headmaster's cottage next to the school, her temporary furnished apartment. She seemed frightened by his presence.

Sensing that, he presented his most sincere smile. He gazed at her bump, which she was absently cradling with both hands.

"Is there anything at all you need?" he asked, playing the role of gracious host. "I hope the stress isn't too difficult."

"No … it's fine."

"I'm so glad."

"Is this about Hugo? Is he alright?"

The preacher nodded. "He's in fine form. In fact, we've been in constant contact."

She relaxed a bit. "Then why are you here?"

"To give you these."

Caprice produced a stack of folded yellow pages that appeared to have been ripped from a notepad. He placed them in the center of the table, then joined Ashley in silent observation for a few moments.

"What is that?" she asked, finally.

"The notes Hugo has sent me. I thought you might like to see them."

Puzzled, she scooped them up and started reading. The messages were a series of demands, written by hand in capital letters.

THESE BED SHEETS AND PILLOWCASES ARE DISGUSTING.
CHANGE THEM AT ONCE!

DO NOT FEED THE MASTIFFS ANYTHING OTHER THAN
THE SPECIAL BLENDS IN THE BUTLER'S PANTRY!

I DEMAND THAT YOU RETURN MY PHONE IMMEDIATELY!
IT IS VITAL THAT I MAINTAIN CONTACT
WITH GALACTIX SPACE DIVISION.

I CANNOT EAT ANOTHER WRETCHED PEANUT BUTTER SANDWICH!
HAVE MY CHEF PREPARE MY MEALS FROM NOW ON!

DID YOU SEE MY MESSAGE ABOUT GALACTIX? IT IS
ABSOLUTELY ESSENTIAL THAT I CONTACT THEM!

RETURN ME TO MY HOME IMMEDIATELY
AND END THIS NONSENSE!!

SEND MY BUTLER TO THE ESTATE TO FETCH NEW CLOTHES.
I HAVE BEEN WEARING THESE FOR TWO DAYS!

I NEED FRESH AIR. I INSIST THAT I BE RELEASED FROM
THIS TERRIBLE ROOM FOR SEVERAL HOURS A DAY!

IS SOMEONE FEEDING THE KOI IN THE LOWER POND?

WHERE IS MY PHONE? I DEMAND IT BE RETURNED AT ONCE!

TAKE ME TO SEE THE DOGS! I MUST KNOW IF THEY ARE OK!

THESE SANDWICHES ARE CRUEL AND UNUSUAL PUNISHMENT!
WHERE IS MY CHEF!

BRING ME MY PHONE!

There were tears in her eyes when she finished reading. Clutching the notes to her chest, she looked at the priest in a hopeful way.

"Did he ask about me?"

"No. I'm sorry."

"Not even once?"

He shook his head sadly.

"I'll leave you alone. It's a lot to think about."

"Why are you doing this? To punish Hugo? Or me?"

Caprice, rising to his feet, took a deep breath. The heartbreak written on this woman's face bothered him more than he'd expected.

"Neither," he said. "You deserve to know. That is all."

TWENTY-EIGHT

BEFORE

"TELL ME MORE about the fragments, Jeremy."

Slivers of memories. Shards from the past. Menacing shadows floating in space.

Stone had been trying to put them together, form some kind of coherent narrative, but that had proved to be an impossible task. No matter how hard he tried, the images and sounds remained disconnected. Seemingly random thoughts and words.

"They're … too splintered," he said. "They don't make sense."

"You have to keep trying," Caprice urged. "When you look closely what do you see?"

Stone took a breath deep enough to fill his lungs. "I'm in a car. It's dark out."

"Go on."

"I'm driving, but I don't know where. I'm tuning into a radio station. I hear music – and a crunch."

"A crunch?"

"Yeah, like I hit something."

"Did you pull over to check?"

"I don't know. That's all I remember."

"Is that typical after a blackout? To have only part of your memory of what transpired restored?"

"Yes. … Sometimes, there's nothing. I don't remember a thing."

"That must be frightening – the not knowing. How have you coped with it in the past?"

"Sometimes, I'd ask the people I went out with what happened. Usually, they'd laugh and tell me just how stinking drunk and rude I got. Other times, they were pissed and told me to go fuck myself."

"And if you went out alone and had only a dim recollection the next morning?"

"I guess I'd hope for the best."

Caprice, revealing no emotion, wrote something in the pad on his lap. "Let's return to your memory about driving. The next day, is there another fragment?"

Stone shrugged. "I can't tell if it was the next day. It could just be a nightmare for all I know. Or something completely unrelated."

"Tell me."

"I was kneeling in front of the car. I remember feeling the grill with my hand. It was dented."

"You hit something."

"There was something else. When I looked at my hand, there was blood."

"That's disturbing. What did you do?"

"I tried to retrace my steps. Drove back to Benny's, the bar where I'd met a couple of friends. I only remember playing pool and drinking beer and shots. The bartender said I left alone around closing time. That's all he knew."

"So, you were drunk and got behind the wheel anyway?"

"Probably," Stone said, shaking his head sadly. "I've done it before."

"And you ran over something on the road. Something that bled."

Stone looked away. "When I tried to figure out what happened, I drove home by the usual route and didn't see anything like a dead animal. Deer are always stepping into the road from the woods there and getting hit by cars."

"I can tell that these fragments worry you, Jeremy."

"Yeah."

"Why?"

"There's another memory. I'm in the car and there's a song playing that I like. I'm turning up the volume. And somehow I can see myself in the rear view singing."

"And then?"

"There's that crunch. And the look in the mirror … changes to pure horror."

"I see," Caprice said. "You don't know what you hit that night. You may never know, and it terrifies you."

"Something like that."

"Did you go to the police? Show them the blood?"

Stone shook his head.

"I thought about that, but I was afraid. I already had a DUI on my record. So, I checked the paper, looking for any accident stories … or obituaries. There weren't any that I could find."

"And what about the front end of the car?"

"I had it fixed. I … I couldn't bear looking at it."

The priest patted Stone on the knee.

"That's all for today, Jeremy. You've come a long way. A very long way."

———

Stone opened the door to the closeted bar for the first time in days.

He stood at the threshold, rigid as a statue.

G'day, Jeremy, the whiskey bottle called out. *I miss ya. We all miss ya!*

"I'm … I'm not listening."

Ah, pour yourself a small one. G'head, m'boy.

Somehow, a cool glass filled his hand.

That's right!

Stone looked down and saw a familiar amber liquid. A tempting double.

The good stuff, Jeremy. Top o' the line.

He raised the glass to his nose, breathed in the rich aromas. So unlike his usual. So complex and inviting. His lips parted in expectation.

Smoooooth as silk. Take a sip and see!

The other bottles formed a chorus.

YOU'LL SEE, JERAMEE!

YOU'LL SEE, JERAMEE!!

The glass dropped to the floor with a crash. Jeremy watched the booze puddle around his feet.

The chanting stopped. The whiskey bottle was angry now. "*Ya feckin' eeeejit! Look what you've done!*"

Stone covered his ears but couldn't shut out the taunts.

He ran out of the house into the street.

And he screamed.

TWENTY-NINE

UPPS WATCHED the protest grow with a practiced eye.

From the mayor's office balcony, he looked down at the knot of demonstrators in the plaza below. There were just a handful at first, waving signs proclaiming TAX THE RICH and ONE PERCENTERS MUST PAY.

Pucci had scoffed at the downtown demonstration, calling it "feeble," but the strategist knew better.

After police shootings in Black communities, he'd seen angry crowds gather quickly, seemingly multiplying out of nowhere, and this protest had that kind of vibe. A flash mob. Powerful, spontaneous and difficult to control.

Within an hour, the crowd had swelled to a few hundred and the noise was loud enough to be heard inside City Hall. Police were scrambling to take positions defending surrounding buildings.

Soon, the mayor's phone was ringing. Protesters were streaming into the city, shutting down afternoon rush-hour traffic. Thousands were now gathering in the plaza and surrounding streets. A makeshift stage was erected. Activists with bullhorns were leading chants.

"Economic justice is racial justice!"

"Say it louder! Economic justice is RACIAL JUSTICE!"

Upps studied the people below and found them to be surprisingly diverse. A large number of college students and activists, for sure, but also moms with young daughters, office workers and laborers. Black, Brown and White, young and old. The full spectrum.

They'd all been inspired by the standoff on Turner Island, of that there was no doubt. The SAVE CAPRICE signs in the crowd spoke volumes.

Pucci stood beside Upps, looking much more anxious than before.

"This isn't good," he whispered.

"No, it isn't."

"Should I have the police break it up?"

"With riot shields and clubs? How about tear gas and rubber bullets?"

"Only if necessary, Upps."

"Look at that," the strategist said, pointing to the TV news trucks on the fringes. "It's all going live, Sal. You're already preparing a military response to the Turner Island situation that could get ugly. Do you really want to start attacking college kids and housewives, too? With the election a few months away?"

"Fair point. But doesn't it make me look weak?"

Upps snorted. "Better to look weak than cause blood to run in the streets."

"I could go down and address them."

"That would only inflame them. Look, I'm not seeing torches and pitchforks. Let the protest run its course. They'll be moving through the city soon. Better get the police in position to protect against broken windows and looting."

"How do you know?"

"Seen it a hundred times."

Sure enough, about 15 minutes later, the protest turned into a march, snaking through the downtown business district. Upps and Pucci watched it unfold on TV.

A reporter asked one of the demonstrators, a 44-year-old drywaller named Wally, why he was there.

"What's happening on the island opened my eyes," he said, pointing toward the water. "Greedy billionaires only thinking about themselves. Getting richer by the day. Never paying their fair share; never giving back. That priest out there is a hero, man."

"What do you think is going to happen to him?"

"They're going to kill him, man. Just like King and the Kennedys."

A woman named Amanda brought her 12-year-old daughter.

"This is a historic moment," the mother said. "This is the day we finally say 'enough is enough' to the greed of the billionaire class. They've enjoyed their free ride at our expense for far too long."

Pucci rubbed his temples. He knew the protests would spread beyond his city, that it would gather steam. The working class and the poor united against the nation's 900 or so billionaires reaping so much wealth.

And the messenger, the messiah, was Caprice.

The man he unwittingly helped build into a potent force.

"This isn't good," he said again. "Not at all."

CHAPTER

THIRTY

AND ON THE seventh day, the third-richest man in America chipped in.

For Sterling, it was ultimately a business decision. He could continue to resist the mounting pressure to contribute to Caprice's fund, or he could quietly relent and return to his magnificent manor, leaving behind his ghastly, smelly digs.

Once the standoff ended, with Caprice and his gang behind bars, Sterling's lawyers would find a way to claw back the $500 million donation, while publicly he would declare empathy for the church's humanitarian mission.

As he sat alone in his grand living room, grumbling about having to make his own cocktail and feed the dogs because the servants were still being detained, he thought about the upcoming launch of the Mars probe and how much he missed his phone and other devices. And then, later, he thought about his wife.

He assumed she'd also be released and allowed to return home, but her absence didn't bother him at the moment. He needed time to think and her constant preening was annoying.

From a massive leather sectional, he turned on a giant TV and watched the news eagerly, like a man who'd been denied basic rations.

His eyebrows shot up when a picture of himself appeared on the screen. It was a publicity shot distributed widely by Galactix that captured his profile nicely.

"One of the nation's richest men, Hugo Sterling, has contributed to the global anti-poverty fund launched during the Turner Island siege, bringing the total to an astonishing $1.1 billion," the newscaster said.

"At least a third of the money has already been distributed to more than a hundred nonprofits in the U.S. and abroad. Experts believe the spending that will follow, including job creation and construction, will be a significant boost to a stagnant economy.

"Jeremy Stone, the only journalist allowed on the island, reported today that the leader of the takeover, Rev. Charles Caprice, said his work is 'nearly completed.' It's unclear whether the group will surrender or force military action to free those still being held.

"In other news …"

Sterling clicked off the TV. He despised the radical priest but admired the way he was manipulating the media, recasting his image. If Caprice was sent to prison now, his base of followers would grow a hundred-fold. If he was to die in a military operation to retake the enclave, he'd be a martyr mourned by millions.

The billionaire made his way upstairs to the safe room and was relieved to see that everything was still there. The jewels, the gold, the stocks and bonds.

After admiring his cherished possessions for a while, he opened the hatch leading to the escape tunnel.

Looking down through the opening, Sterling thought about making a run for it, getting on a WaveRunner and heading straight for the nearest police boat. But would they know it was him? Might the snipers open fire?

He stood there, weighing options like the astute businessman he was, when a familiar voice broke the silence.

"Thinking of leaving without me?"

Ashley Sterling was standing just inside the thick vault door, a fierceness in her eyes. He stepped over to embrace her, but she didn't return the hug.

"How are you, my love?" he asked.

"*Am* I your love, Hugo? Or is this your true love? Your glittering treasure."

He reached for her cheek, but she brushed his hand away.

"They gave me all your urgent notes," she said, words dripping with acid. "The ones you wrote every day while we were separated. You demanded better food. You demanded better linens. You insisted on proper feeding of the dogs. Even the stinking koi. But, not once, my darling, did you ask about me."

"Oh, my love, I thought about you constantly!"

"Do you know where I was being held? Did you even ask?"

"They wouldn't have told me," he said in a whisper.

Her dry, unpainted lips curled into a savage smile.

"That's funny, because they answered *my* questions. I asked about you every day. Where you were, whether you were alright, whether I could see you. Every night, I cried for you. Did you shed any tears for me, Hugo?"

"Of course, my sweet."

"Fuck you," she snarled. "Stay in the guest cottage. I don't want to see your lying face ever again."

———

When Fallone didn't return, Weathers began fearing the worst.

While she'd developed an understanding with Caprice, she feared the bodyguard with the shark eyes. He looked like the sort who enjoyed inflicting pain.

She left the house to get answers and was relieved to find the priest at his usual meditation spot, the park bench. His eyes were closed but his lips were moving, perhaps uttering a silent prayer.

As she approached, he smiled.

"Ah, Cicely," he said, looking up at her with those glowing eyes.

"Sorry to disturb your … meditation."

"Please sit with me. I was just ending my conversation. I would like to start another."

Weathers looked around. They were very much alone, except for the occasional gliding gull and dashing squirrel.

"Conversation?"

Caprice smiled. "With God. I can hear him most clearly here, beside the trees and flowers. The cherry trees, by the way, will bloom next spring. Please don't cut them down."

"That's what you talked about? *Trees?*"

"Not with Him. Trees are gentle creatures that communicate through the rustle of their leaves and the sap flowing through their trunk and branches, if you listen very closely. Tap into the current, if you will. It's a skill I have spent years trying to master. I have a long way to go, I'm afraid. But these trees are very much alive."

"Someday you'll have to teach me," Weathers said, although she was really thinking something else. *The tree whisperer. Are you kidding me?*

"What brings you here?" he asked.

"Joey Fallone. What have you done with him?"

"I can see that he's more than an employee to you. Also, your close friend?"

"Yes, a friend. Please answer my question."

"We have him under lock and key, but I've told Langston he is not to be harmed in any way. We simply can't have him running around, meddling in our affairs. We're at a delicate stage, Cicely. Thanks to your assistance, we've met our fundraising goal. The monies are being distributed, but we need more time to finish the job."

"Why does Joey threaten any of that? I don't understand."

The priest paused, debating whether to say anything more.

"May I talk to you in confidence?" he asked.

"Yes."

"The reason people are still being held in the school is because we are bluffing. The police believe we have explosives and will blow up the building with everyone inside if they attempt to retake the island. None of that is true, of course. We just need to have them believe it, so we have the time to finish our work here."

"And Joey was about to report that there are no bombs?"

"Exactly. So, you see, we have no choice but to detain him."

"May I see him?"

"Of course. Anything else?"

"Can you release the older residents? Some have conditions that require medication. Please let them go home."

The preacher thought for a moment. "That's a kind and reasonable request. Anyone with a serious medical condition will be released," he declared.

"Thank you."

Caprice raised his right hand and, seemingly out of nowhere, Langston appeared, grim-faced as always.

"My friend, let's reassure Ms. Weathers. Take her to Mr. Fallone."

Then he closed his eyes and resumed his meditation.

———

"Put me on that damn island!"

McCoy was in the mayor's office, the chief at his side. The detective had been reading the three texts from Fallone over and over. There was something wrong about them. The word choices. The stiffness. The complete sentences with periods.

Fallone was from a rough-and-tumble Italian neighborhood in Philly and didn't speak like that. He butchered grammar and spelling, used as many abbreviations as possible, and sprinkled in a few expletives.

The texts were just too clean, the detective concluded. They'd likely caught Fallone and were using his phone to spread misinformation. There were no bombs. The crates in the trucks were fakes.

"That's an interesting theory, detective," Pucci said. "But if you're wrong, people could die."

"Put me on the island," McCoy pleaded. "One man can get through undetected. Give me a goddamn canoe and I'll get the proof we need."

"And if you're caught? Then we've put those people in even more jeopardy."

"I won't get caught. Christ, Fallone was running around undetected for days. They don't have enough men to patrol the entire shoreline."

The chief nodded. "That's true, Sal. We can use the drones to guide him to an unguarded location. He goes to the school, checks it out, slips back out. At least we'll finally know what we're dealing with."

Pucci wished Upps was around. He'd know what to do, politically speaking.

"Seems risky." He looked over at McCoy. "This man Caprice, who knows how he might retaliate if you're captured."

"I won't be."

"It's crucial intel," Winterbrook said.

The mayor paused to mull it over. His entire political life had been filled with calculated risks, and this proposed, possibly suicidal one-man mission was merely the latest to cross his desk.

Perhaps the biggest risk of all, though, was not taking decisive action. Looking weak and vulnerable. Looking scared.

"Okay, McCoy, you've convinced me," he said in a low voice. "Go out there tonight."

———

Bridget and Barry were packed and ready to go.

They'd convinced all three of their wayward clients to contribute substantially to the fund, using their considerable powers of persuasion and charm. They'd delivered. Now they wanted off the island.

They'd sent a note to Caprice, informing him of their success and their desire to leave, as quickly as possible. The fixers had no intention of being around when the soldiers stormed in.

When the knock came, Bridget smoothed her dress and fluffed her hair. Caprice would be grateful, she knew. He'd provide an escort to the bridge, and from there, at last, to safety. It had been an unpleasant situation, but it was over.

She opened the door and saw only Langston. Her thousand-watt smile dimmed.

"You can't leave," he said in his usual monolithic way.

Bridget glanced at Barry, who was holding his garment bag, ready to go. He looked stunned.

"We did everything he asked. We even made a personal donation," Bridget implored. "We need to leave."

"You'll stay here like everyone else," Langston said.

Bridget, her eyes watering, began to tremble.

"But the soldiers are coming. What are we supposed to do?"

Langston's poker face crumbled. In its place was a big smile. His eyes, usually so dark, twinkled just a bit.

"Pray," he said.

THIRTY-ONE

FOR THE FIRST time, Caprice entered the school.

As he strode through the gymnasium, past the rows of cots, he said nothing. He could feel the primal mix of fear and hate coursing through the room, and it made him uncomfortable, even a little sad. He had devoted years of his life to easing such emotions.

From the elevated stage on the far side of the room, he waved for the innocents he'd imprisoned to come closer.

"You'll want to hear what I have to say," he said in his sermon voice, loud enough to render a microphone unnecessary. "Those of you in the back, move up please."

The detainees, a mix of young and old, male and female, surged forward, prompting Langston to adopt a defensive stance. Feet pointed forward. Head on a swivel. Hand at his side, inches from the gun hidden by his now unbuttoned blazer.

He was the reverend's only protector, but he was enough.

"There, that's better."

"Let us go!" one man shouted, triggering a wave of nods and murmurs.

Caprice held up his hands and the crowd hushed.

"That is exactly why I'm here, if you will allow me to explain," he said. "It has pained me to keep you here, away from the comfort of your homes. In some cases, away from your loved ones and friends on the mainland. Please believe me when I tell you there was no other way."

He pointed at the TVs that had been brought in, commandeered from their homes, to keep the people informed.

"As you are no doubt aware, the police are threatening to take the island back by force. The only thing stopping them is you. You see, we believe in the power of the Lord. We are not a militant group. We have no assault weapons, no rocket launchers. We have been defending the barricade with sticks and stones. Yes, sticks and stones.

"If the police knew that we are powerless to stop them, they would have already attacked. So, I have led them to believe otherwise. But contrary to speculation on the TV news, your lives have never been at risk. That is the truth. We just needed to buy enough time to complete God's work on behalf of the poor. I want to thank you all for helping us do that."

Caprice saw looks of confusion in the crowd and gave his best reassuring smile.

"Our work is drawing to a close, my friends. Very soon, hopefully within the next 24 hours, you'll all be able to resume your lives. The barricade will come down and the highway will reopen. Life on the island will return to normal and nobody, not a single soul, will have been seriously hurt."

For the first time, he smiled. His cat eyes glowed.

"Please accept my sincerest apology for the inconvenience all of this has caused. Goodnight and may God be with us in these final hours."

He was leaving the stage with Langston at his side when a terrible roar suddenly filled the room. The wood floor trembled in an ominous way.

"We're under attack!" someone yelled.

The roar faded, then returned a couple of minutes later, even louder this time. The hanging lights began to swing.

Two men rushed over to Langston with an urgent message. The big man nodded and whispered in Caprice's ear.

The reverend looked around at the fearful faces. "They're just flexing their muscles. Nothing to worry about," he said.

"Let us go," one woman implored. "Before it's too late!"

"We're sitting ducks in here," the man next to her said.

"There's nothing to worry about," Caprice said, raising his hands for silence once more. "They know that this building is being used to house people. They won't attack here, of all places. Please be patient for just a little while longer."

As the thunder from the fly-over faded, he left the room in his usual brisk pace.

"Military choppers. They're testing our defenses, Father," Langston said when they were outside. "They'll be attacking at first light."

"Where are we on the money transfers?"

"About three-quarters done."

"Let's step it up. Increase the size of the grants," Caprice said, patting his bodyguard on the back. "Spend every penny. Leave the authorities nothing."

———

When Langston brought Weathers to the Turner Island Yacht Club, she wondered if it was some kind of sick joke.

The exclusive club on the water's edge was where the more sociable billionaires would unwind over cocktails, caviar and fresh oysters on the half shell, bragging about their latest acquisitions and mergers, and regaling one another with accounts of lavish travels and boastful recaps of the newest and most expensive cosmetic surgery.

Weathers wasn't a member, although she and her husband had once been invited to join. She just found the atmosphere too stuffy for her taste. Even the professional waiters, in their black bowties, seemed more robotic than human.

She was almost relieved when Langston directed her down into the basement, where drums of heating oil, racks of firewood, barrels of imported whiskey and boxes of kitchen supplies were stored. Outside a windowless steel door, he stopped.

"I need to do a check," Langston said. "Put your arms out."

He frisked her roughly, then unlatched the black door.

"Five minutes."

"Caprice didn't say that."

"Yeah, well, I'm in charge of security. Five minutes. I'll be right outside."

She entered the small room with its concrete floor and walls as Fallone rose from the cot. He smiled as the door clanged shut.

"Cicely."

"Joey. Have they hurt you?"

"No, I'm okay."

There was a simple wood chair in the room. Like a good host, Fallone set it before Weathers.

"That loud noise a few minutes ago. What was it?" he asked as he returned to the edge of the bed, and she settled on the chair.

"Three helicopters going back and forth. I could see the pilots, they were so low."

"I think they're about to make their move, Cicely. Things could get a little hairy. You better move into the safe room until things settle down. It's well stocked. I checked last week."

"I'm more worried about you, Joey."

"I'm okay in this basement," he said, patting the wall, cold as a crypt. He wasn't going to tell her about Langston's plan to make him walk the DMZ like a suicidal man.

"I have to leave," she said tenderly. "I'll ask Caprice to let you go. He's reasonable, I think."

"Promise me you'll be in the safe room tonight. I'll come get you when it's over."

"I promise."

They stood in the room and held hands, staring into each other's eyes.

Then they embraced for what seemed like a very long time.

———

McCoy cut the electric motor, using the aluminum oars to guide the inflatable boat silently to the shore.

With his black face paint and dark green camo uniform, he looked like a Navy Seal or assassin. He pulled the Zodiac into some bushes. Then he checked his new gun, making sure it was loaded.

"On the beach. No sign of patrols," he whispered into his radio. "Switching off until the job is done. Over and out."

It was a good idea to use the helicopters as a noisy diversion. They buzzed the island just as he was approaching the shore. All eyes would have been looking up, not out, for those crucial moments.

There was a half moon shining down, which wasn't ideal, but he'd have to take that chance. Weaving through bushes and trees, he made his way to the school in the heart of the island.

There was only one sentry by the door, and just one person walking the perimeter. McCoy waited until that guard passed, then made his way to the 7-foot-high stone wall that ringed the school. There were no signs of any wires or charges.

He followed the roaming guard at a safe distance, covering the entire perimeter. Nothing alarming at all, but he'd need to check around the entrance to be certain.

That's when he saw Langston, the burly bodyguard who'd given him a beating, walking with a woman. He recognized her as the mouthpiece for the island, the one Fallone was paid to protect.

Langston called for the sentry at the door to come over.

"Take her straight home," he commanded. "No more stops."

"Yes, sir."

McCoy watched with relief as Langston disappeared into the shadows. He'd prefer not to have another bruising encounter with the enforcer.

In a stroke of good fortune, the entrance to the school was unguarded – at least for a few minutes. The detective ran over, bouncing from tree to tree. He searched for signs of explosives, finding nothing.

Carefully, lest he alert any guards positioned in the inner courtyard, he opened the door. He scooted along the inside of the wall until he reached a play field on the south end of the school. Then he doubled back to the gym where people were being held. Not a single sign of any bombs.

He checked his watch and saw that he'd been on the island for 31 minutes. He'd promised to report back within the hour. The chief and the mayor would want a briefing.

It was time to leave, but he wished he could take Joey with him. Based on his own experience with Langston, he was probably being beaten – or worse.

Hang in there, buddy.

McCoy found a tree to climb that would allow him to get over the rock wall. He dropped to the ground on the other side, checked to see if anyone was watching, then sprinted toward the beach grateful for the darkness.

Minutes later, he was back in the Zodiac headed for a waiting police boat.

"No signs of explosives," he said, radioing in. "The school is clear. I repeat, the school is clear."

THIRTY-TWO

FROM HIS FAMILIAR perch in the park, Caprice felt a gentle breeze scented by flowers tenderly massage his face. The sky was a gorgeous, unblemished blue.

And an army was coming for him.

For the past hour, they'd been massing on the bridge: armored bulldozers, troop carriers and tanks, and several hundred National Guard members dressed for war. Helicopters bristling with .50-caliber machine guns had been swooping across the slender island, rattling windows and everyone's nerves.

Caprice, though, smiled.

"My friend, I couldn't have done any of this without you," he told Langston. "We've set an example of generosity and compassion for generations to follow."

"Yes, Father."

"Has the fund been emptied?"

"The final grant was wired 20 minutes ago. An anti-hunger network in Burundi that meets your requirements."

"Excellent. Have you instructed our people to surrender? Not to resist in any way?"

"Yes, Father. What should we do with the people in the school?"

"It's safer if they stay together, I think. I don't want them roaming the island when it's under attack. Please have someone check on our wandering boy as well."

"And Fallone? Release him like we did the detective?"

Father sighed. "Much as I hate to meddle in your amusements, I stopped by last night and unlocked the door. He's served his purpose."

Langston nodded stiffly, looking like a child who'd just had his favorite toy taken away.

"Well, I suppose it's time to pay a final visit to Mr. Sterling," Caprice said, rising from his bench. "I must hear his confession. I can go alone, if you'd prefer."

"No, I'd like to be there. We've come this far."

"Of course."

"Father?"

"Yes, my friend?"

"I won't let them hurt you. If they open fire, I'll take the bullet."

"I know you will, my dear Langston. I know."

———

Stone watched in amazement as the men at the barricade simply walked away.

In the end, it had all been an elaborate bluff. There would be no resistance by the faithful. Not a single shot fired. No bombs exploding.

Caprice's takeover of Billionaire Island had gone exactly as he'd planned.

Stone knew at that moment that he'd been played, coaxed into performing his role as the cynical journalist in the midst of the standoff. He was credible to the outside world precisely because he wasn't one of the radicals, and Caprice knew it.

The reporter set out to find the priest, ask him some questions. He jogged to the school and saw it was no longer being guarded. All of the People's Oasis followers were gathering a couple of blocks away, on the lawn at the park.

For eight days, they had held the people on the island captive and the police at bay. Now, they were all looking serene, as if headed to a family picnic. Their heavenly duty was over, moving them that much closer to God.

Following them, Stone witnessed a stirring spectacle. All of the believers began kneeling on the grass to pray. The ancient chanted words reached him, giving him goosebumps.

He began filling pages in his notebook.

In the margin, he wrote: "Where's Caprice??"

———

Dinwittie had a lump in his throat as the tank rolled past, clanking slowly up the bridge.

"Damn, it's beautiful," he said as armored personnel carriers filled with soldiers followed the tank. "American firepower at work."

Dinwittie had his helmet on, binoculars hanging around his neck. He waited for the blast of the tank's cannon, but there was none.

Instead, the perplexed soldier standing in the machine gun turret radioed something strange.

"They're gone," he said. "Nobody's here."

The commander's face grew red. How could he be denied his glory?

His shining moment?

"That can't be!" he yelled at the captain awaiting his orders. "Send in the troops!"

They poured out of the rear of the transports and spread out, assault rifles at the ready. They reached the barrier without firing a shot.

There was nothing but a pile of rocks and tree branches cut to resemble rifles. One soldier stood atop the makeshift wall. Shrugging, he waved one of the sticks.

Dinwittie cursed and headed down the bridge with the rest of the soldiers. Maybe the zealots were planning a final stand at the school, he thought. Yes, they must have regrouped and taken up defensive positions there.

There was still a battle to be won.

That notion lifted his spirits. He quickened his pace.

"C'mon soldiers," he called out. "We still have work to do."

———

Fallone was ready.

Before dawn, he'd managed to break one of the legs off the chair, muffling the snap with his shirt. When his captors entered the cell to drag him to the barricade, he intended to club them senseless and make his escape.

But hours passed, and nobody came.

When he heard a distant rumbling that he took to be an approaching army, he began to fret. The last thing he wanted was to be trapped in a basement following a barrage of artillery fire.

He pounded on the steel door.

"Hey, shitheads! Get me outta here!"

Fallone pounded again, yelling louder, but there was no response. He put his ear to the door and heard nothing.

Then he tried the latch. The door opened without a struggle, causing Fallone's jaw to drop. There wasn't a guard in sight. Even weirder: His borrowed phone was resting on one of the stools.

"What the heck?"

The rumbling was getting louder. He scrambled up the stairs and caught a glimpse of soldiers, dozens of them, moving inland. He needed to get ahead of them, make it to Billionaire's Row before hell was unleashed.

He was no longer doing his job.

But he longed to protect Cicely just the same.

———

When word reached the mayor that the operation was going smoothly, meeting no resistance, he smiled for the first time in a long while.

"Join me for a drink, Upps," he told his strategist.

"Isn't it a tad early? Possibly premature?"

"All of the people in that damn school have been rescued. Not a single person harmed. No, I'd say a toast is very much in order."

Upps laughed and accepted a pour of single-malt Scotch. They clinked glasses.

"What about Caprice?"

Pucci leaned back in his chair with a satisfied look. "He'll turn up. They're going down Billionaire's Row as we speak."

Upps swirled the expensive booze in his glass and took a sip, raising his eyebrows appreciatively.

"That deal you offered the priest," he said. "Probation, no prison. Are you still considering it?"

"Hell no. I want that bastard behind bars."

"Even though he did apparently stand down in the end?"

"That SOB kept me between a rock and a hard place for more than a week," Pucci said. "Now he pays the price. I'll press the DA to seek a maximum sentence."

Upps nodded.

"With a successful end to the world's most publicized standoff, and a conviction of the ringleader, you can punch your own ticket, Sal. Maybe the governor's office."

Pucci gave his advisor a wink.

"I like the sound of that," he said. "*Governor.*"

THIRTY-THREE

THE LIBERATION of the Turner Island captives didn't require great military skill. Nor courage.

Thanks to Cavill, the islanders had already formed a line with hands raised over their heads before the soldiers poured in.

The released prisoners walked calmly outside, looking somewhat bemused at the presence of a small army, including a very large tank idling lazily outside Tranquility Cove.

The medics who'd rushed to the front shrugged. There was nothing to do.

"We were treated well," Cavill told them. "Some of the older residents are a bit sore from sleeping on cots. There were some complaints about not being allowed outside, that sort of thing. But all of that is now in the past. We're happy that it's over."

That sentiment was corroborated a short time later, when laughter filled the streets. Within minutes, champagne was being uncorked. Barbecue grills were wheeled out to the sidewalk. Pets that had apparently been cared for by the occupiers joined the celebration.

A block party was underway and The Wiz was playing tunes again.

The only islander displeased with the turn of events was Frankie, who'd been reunited with his long-tormented housekeeper.

The spontaneous music and cheers infuriated Dinwittie, who refused to give up all hope of a much-deserved rise to a general's rank.

There was still a chance that the final stand of the bad guys would be on Billionaire's Row.

He ordered his soldiers to press on to the far end of the island.

———

Sterling was in a daze.

His wife of five years had just announced her intention to seek a divorce, which should have been more cleaving than it was. He should have been weeping, or something like that, he knew. Or perhaps at her feet, begging for forgiveness. Basic human emotions.

He felt none of that. Had she been more of a possession than a life partner? Was she now more or less a lost material object? One of his disposable assets?

The billionaire many times over was shaking his head, trying to make sense of it all, when Caprice and Langston entered the guest cottage – itself a grand enough residence to be considered a mansion.

"Hugo, you seem troubled," the reverend said.

"None of your business."

"Quite true, and I hate to interfere with your reflection, but there is something I need from you."

Sterling looked at the priest and scowled. "I paid your blood money. Screw off."

"Indeed, you did," Caprice said calmly. "The final contribution. Your gift to the malnourished in several African countries. Is that right, Langston?"

The bodyguard tipped his head.

"I'll get it all back, every cent, when you and your goons are rotting in prison."

"So, you never intended to help others with your money?"

"Hell no! They can all fuck themselves. The poor, the homeless, the addicts you're so infatuated with – we'd all be better off if they were wiped off the face of the Earth."

Caprice studied the billionaire, like an epidemiologist with a pathogen, for a long minute. Of all the people on the island, Sterling was the most consumed by status and wealth. He practically reeked of it.

Such a pity.

To Langston, the priest said simply, "Bring him."

Ten minutes later, Caprice stood in the vast master bathroom, with its Italian marble and fixtures coated in real gold, and whistled in astonishment. A dozen homeless people could shelter here, he thought.

Sterling stumbled inside, pushed by Langston.

"Hugo, how nice of you to join me. I was just about to reveal that marvelous treasure room of yours. The one mentioned in that article in Architectural Digest."

Sterling responded with a raspy laugh that sounded like a chainsaw cutting. "You'll never find it," he scoffed. "Not in a hundred years."

Caprice smiled, resembling a patient father dealing with a tempestuous toddler.

"Do you remember a man named William Carpetti?" he asked.

Sterling folded his arms and glared.

"No? He served you for five years as a construction supervisor. Mr. Carpetti injured his back rather severely working on your home and had to go on medical leave. Still not ringing any bells?

"Anyway, Mr. Carpetti became severely addicted to the hundreds of opioid painkillers he was prescribed and, sad to say, wound up losing everything. His home, his livelihood, even his family. In the end he was living on the streets, which is where I met him. After I helped him through detox, he shared some very interesting stories about this estate and that safe room of yours in particular. That's why I know exactly where it is, Hugo."

Caprice stepped over to the mirror hanging by the tub, ran his right hand along the frame and stopped about midway down the side.

"Ah, there it is."

With a buzz, the mirror began to rise. Langston, who had a firm hand in the small of Sterling's back, grinned.

"Judgment Day is here," Caprice said, turning to Sterling. "Time to gauge the depths of your depravity and determine your penance."

"You're insane."

"Am I? Tell me, Hugo, have you ever given back? With your great wealth, have you ever given a hand to the people who are suffering, the millions and millions on the bottom rungs of society?"

Sterling pursed his lips, saying nothing.

"Surely, you can remember. I'll tell you what, let's make it easy. Give me just one example. One donation over your entire lifetime that helped others who weren't already wealthy."

"I refuse to play this game."

"Game? This isn't a game, Hugo. This is your life. You've done very, very well for yourself. A true self-made man, yes? But not once have you given back to the millions of people who are suffering. That's a sin, if ever there was one, but I'm going to give you a final chance to demonstrate newfound repentance.

"Open your vault, so we may assess your greed; your idolatry of money. Let us see the golden calf that you worship every single day. Open your vault, Hugo."

"Not a chance," Sterling said bitterly. "The police are coming. They're going to stuff you in a cell, where you'll rot for the rest of your stinking life."

"One last time. Give me the code. Langston is not a patient man."

Despite the hand tightening around his neck, the billionaire seethed. *"I won't!"*

A woman's voice suddenly filled the room.

"But I will," Ashley Sterling said coolly.

Ignoring her whimpering husband, she stepped to the keypad and entered the sequence of numbers, causing the heavy door to spring open with a series of metallic clicks. Then she faced the oversized safe that held the gold, cash and stock certificates and did the same.

One last time, she gazed at the diamonds that had so entranced her. They were shining like a starry night sky, but the spell had been shattered.

"Give it away, for all I care," she told Caprice before striding out. "It makes me sick."

PART 3

ROBIN HOOD

CHAPTER

THIRTY-FOUR

BEFORE

"WHAT HAVE YOU learned, Jeremy?"

Tears were rolling down Stone's cheeks. The therapy was forcing him to put the shards together, and as the puzzle grew more complete so was his feeling of dread.

"I … I may have hit someone. *Killed* someone," he whispered.

"The memory is getting clearer?" Caprice asked gently.

Stone nodded. "Yes … maybe. I remember getting out of the car now. Seeing the damage … and something else. Something lying on the road."

"What do you see?"

"It's not clear. It could be a large carcass or a body."

"I see. Well, if it's an animal, that's unfortunate. But if it's a human being, that's another thing entirely."

"I know! I know!" Stone snapped, wiping away tears.

Caprice leaned back in his chair. He put his pen down.

"I believe this incident is one of the root causes of your addiction, Jeremy. The suicide, of course. But also this. If we can expose it fully to the light, unearth its secrets, it could very well set you free."

Stone's head drooped, but the preacher seemed animated.

"Let's return to the day after, when you saw the damage to the front of the car, the blood on the grill. You say you checked the paper and there was no news about a fatal accident."

"That's right."

"Did you check again?"

"No."

"Are you sure?"

"Yes. Why?"

"A man *was* killed on that very same road. At night, in an apparent hit and run. The story didn't make the paper for several days because the body had apparently been rolled into a gulley lined with thick bushes. But the coroner estimated the time of death to be the night you were drunk and headed home."

Stone looked up at the priest with terror-filled eyes. He felt a white-hot panic rising inside him.

"Are you saying I murdered someone?"

"Not intentionally. But it is possible that you killed someone, I'm afraid."

"And you've known this? For how long?"

"Since you revealed your partial recollection. I did some checking of my own. I'm sorry, Jeremy. It's a lot for you to deal with."

"Who was he?"

"An old war veteran who lived by himself in a cabin nearby. His name was Leo Daniels. He was returning home after volunteering at a shelter, according to the paper."

"Jesus."

"If you had gone to the police, they likely would have tied you to Daniels' death."

"And they'd have charged me with vehicular homicide. Put me in prison."

"Possibly. But at least you would have voluntarily come forward. That counts for something in a court of law. And in the eyes of God."

"I wasn't trying to hide. I … I just didn't know. What should I do, Father?"

"Search your soul," Caprice said. "That's always a good place to start."

———

Killing a man is a very hard thing to deal with.

Jeremy Devon Stone became haunted by it.

He'd looked up the information about Daniels, saw the picture that ran with his obituary. That was the unsmiling face, under a Marine's desert camo hat and buzz cut, that spooked Stone almost every night. His eyes could be open or shut, it didn't seem to matter.

Sometimes, Daniels would appear by the foot of his bed and simply ask *why* over and over and over. Stone would wake, his mouth twisted in a scream, the sheets soaked with sweat.

In hopes of easing his torment, he looked up the man's brother, who lived a hundred miles away in a rural area. He drove out to the home, a pleasant country farmhouse with chickens in the yard, but couldn't knock on the door.

Hours passed with him sitting in his car – the killing machine – wondering how he could start a conversation with the victim's family. "Hello, I'm Jeremy. I killed your brother because I was stinking drunk."

Stone drove back to the city feeling overwhelming grief and despair, a suffocating blanket. He struggled to breathe. To think.

And, yes, he wanted whiskey. A whole fifth.

He'd completed his counseling with Caprice a couple of weeks earlier and was attending AA meetings, yet he felt he was being held together by mere threads. He became increasingly paranoid, convinced he was being followed by plainclothes detectives in unmarked sedans.

Stone started taking offramps at the last second, making sudden U-turns in traffic, speeding up and braking hard – just to see if he could expose the undercover cops.

From his bedroom window, he'd spy on the cars parked below, jotting down descriptions in his notebook. Once, when he was walking back from the grocery store, he saw a man pull up in a black SUV and became convinced he was the one he'd seen following him earlier in the day.

He went up to the window and gave it a tap. "Are you watching me? Huh? Are you?"

The man, perhaps used to crazies, merely pointed at the Uber placard on the dash. Seconds later, his fare materialized – an elderly woman with a cane.

Stone mumbled an apology and walked away. He was losing it.

Back in his apartment, pacing the living room, he decided to call Betters. She'd calm him down, help him think straight. She always did.

"Hello, Jeremy," she said. "I haven't gotten your story. Is the check in the mail?"

Stone had completely forgotten about the story he'd been working on for the past three weeks. Well, not entirely. It's just impossible to give writing the attention it deserved when a ghost was on the loose. He wanted desperately to tell his editor that.

"Sally, I'll get it to you soon, I promise. I've hammered out a rough draft."

"Oh yeah? Only it's too rough to share." There wasn't an excuse that Betters hadn't heard before.

"That's right. Look, I'm calling because I think I may have done something really bad."

"Like what?"

"Hit someone with my car."

"Hit someone? Like when you were drinking?"

"Yeah. I couldn't remember anything until I started doing counseling with Caprice. He got me to piece it together. I think I may have killed a man at night when he was crossing the road."

"Christ, Jeremy. What are you going to do?"

"Go to the police, I guess."

"That may be premature. You don't want to confess to something unless you're 100 percent sure. How sure are you?"

Stone sighed heavily. "I don't know. A man named Leo Daniels was struck and killed in a hit-and-run the night I left a bar in a haze. All I can remember is that I hit *something*. The grill of my car was damaged when I looked at it the next day. Until Caprice, I thought it was probably just a deer."

"I don't trust Caprice, Jeremy. He's not a licensed therapist. He may be messing with your memories in a way that can do you more harm than good."

Stone saw Daniels standing in the corner and had to turn his body to avoid seeing the shimmering specter.

"Yeah, I … I'm not doing too well, Sally."

"Stay away from Caprice. Don't do anything rash, and, for God's sake, don't go out drinking."

There was a long pause that hung heavy in the space between them.

"Sorry about the story," Stone said in a low voice. "I don't really have a rough draft."

"I know, Jeremy."

———

McHenry watched the reporter stagger to his car outside Benny's and actually considered intervening for a fleeting moment.

He could have given the drunk SOB a lift, but wouldn't that have amounted to interference? And if he interfered, wouldn't that cause ripples in the time-space continuum, or some such bullshit?

He'd watched Stone get hammered in the bar, downing shot after shot. His friends had long since peeled off, but he lingered on his stool until closing time.

Finally, he was outside, fumbling with his keys and leaning heavily against the Subaru. It was winter and his breath could be seen in small clouds of steam.

McHenry knew that Stone lived only a few miles away, but the route he took went through a small forested area, with a thousand-foot climb and a series of sharp curves. Blind spots galore. Two-lane road. No lights.

As the Subaru lurched out of the parking lot, McHenry followed in his invisible car. Stone swerved across both lanes with only his parking lights on, but somehow managed to survive the first mile.

In the woods, though, the mist suddenly morphed into a dense fog that reduced visibility to a couple of car lengths. Stone should have slowed down. Instead, he appeared to speed up.

Cursing, McHenry did the same in order to keep pace. Then he saw a glimmer of red up ahead. Brake lights. Stone had come to a complete stop, leaving his car in the middle of the road.

McHenry pulled onto the shoulder and dimmed his headlights. Then he grabbed his camera and crept along the side of the road until he could see the front end of the Subaru. The grill was dented in. A young deer was lying still on the road.

Stone was babbling to himself, pulling the fallen creature to the shoulder. He got back behind the wheel and drove off, forcing McHenry to sprint to his car.

"Goddamnit! That fucker's going to kill himself," he said.

He stepped on the gas, hoping to find the Subaru again, but the fog had become thicker and wetter. There was another curve and he struggled to take it cleanly.

Just as the curve ended, a man appeared in the road.

"Wha-?"

McHenry slammed on his brakes, but the car skidded on the wet pavement. There was a sickly thud. The man disappeared under the hood.

His pulse racing, McHenry backed up and saw the body. It was an older man with a white beard, wearing jeans and hiking boots. His eyes were fixed and glazed. There was no question he was dead.

McHenry shook his head. If anyone should have been in this position, it should have been Stone – shit-faced and driving on a fog-shrouded night. *A true menace.*

He snapped several photos of the body, then dragged the corpse into a brush-lined gulley.

Damned if he was going to take the blame for this, he thought.

Not when he had the perfect patsy.

THIRTY-FIVE

AS THE SOLDIERS scoured Billionaire's Row, hunting for Caprice and his lieutenant, Stone headed straight for Sterling's mansion.

All along, the preacher had taken aim at the recalcitrant resident, whom he viewed as the single greatest symbol of greed in America. The reporter sensed that the standoff would end on the Sterling estate, perhaps in a violent manner.

Stone had taped handmade signs to his shirt declaring PRESS in large capital letters, hoping to avoid being mistaken for one of Caprice's followers. Even so, he kept nervously glancing back over his shoulder. The weekend warriors were far too young and inexperienced to be trusted.

He entered the sprawling grounds through the open security gate and walked past the empty guard booth. The lawn and shrubs, normally groomed to perfection, were now looking strangely wild.

The twin front doors weren't locked. He stepped into the massive foyer with its 25-foot-high ceiling, gleaming marble floor and luxuriously framed original Renaissance paintings. A resplendent crystal chandelier, as big as a car, was the centerpiece.

"Anyone here? It's me, Stone."

He thought he heard a noise coming from above, so he began slowly climbing the grand, curving staircase. As he neared the top, Langston's scowling face suddenly loomed in front of him.

The man was big enough to completely block the way, causing Stone to stop.

"Where's Father?" he asked.

"He's busy."

"The soldiers are coming."

"I know."

"Can I talk to him?"

Langston was about to reply when Caprice called out. "It's okay, Langston. Let him up."

Stone found Caprice in the safe room, inspecting its contents.

"Avarice," the reverend said, shaking his head. "It's rather stunning, isn't it, Jeremy?"

Stone surveyed the contents of the room. He'd never seen such riches.

"Must be worth a fortune."

"Many millions, I presume."

"I can't believe Sterling is letting you take it."

"He's not. The vault was opened by his wife. A woman scorned, as they say."

"Even so, soldiers are right outside. They'll make you put everything back."

"Perhaps," the preacher said, turning up his palms. "Perhaps not."

He opened the display case and began placing the jewelry in a zippered nylon duffle bag.

"I'll … I'll report about this," Stone said. "I'll tell the world what you're doing."

One at a time, Caprice removed the necklaces, pendants and brooches, pausing to admire their quality. The gems and diamonds sparkled like fire.

"And what am I doing, Jeremy?"

"You're stealing! All this high-minded rhetoric about ending poverty – it was all a load of crap. In the end, you're nothing but a common burglar."

Caprice moved on to Sterling's collection of gold objects, ranging from rare coins to stamped bars.

"Ah, you disappoint me, Jeremy. Do burglars give to the needy?"

"They do if it's all a cover for a heist."

"A heist? Is that what you think this is?"

"You should see yourself. Loading a bag with loot. Looking to sneak out before the cops come. How noble."

Caprice flicked Stone a grin. "I invited you up here, to this vault, so you could witness the final chapter. Please don't get the facts wrong."

"I'll expose you and this whole crazy scheme of yours."

The preacher stopped and looked sternly at Stone.

"Will you? Will you risk your reputation and freedom?"

"What are you talking about?"

"I'm talking about vehicular homicide. I'm talking about a photo showing your car at the scene of the crime, the body clearly visible."

"Bullshit."

"Show him, Langston."

The enforcer, once again appearing out of nowhere, handed Stone an envelope. The reporter opened it and saw a photo inside. It was exactly what Caprice had said. Stone's battered car and a man's body lying nearby. He knew from his nightmares that it was Daniels.

"Jesus ... you really were following me."

"Of course," Caprice said. "I knew I could trust you to play your part during the standoff, spreading my message of equality. Thank you for that. But in the end, I also knew you'd be standing here, being the virtuous journalist."

"All those weeks of counseling, drilling into my head. Why?"

"Simple, really. You had to realize that you killed someone. Your protective walls had to come down. But you believe now, don't you? I can see from the look in your eyes that you do. Keep the photo. The original will be sent to the police if you write about our little chat. Now, if you'll excuse me, I have work to do."

Langston grabbed Stone's arm and spun him like a top toward the stairs. When they reached the foyer, the bodyguard cursed. Helmeted men with rifles were moving onto the grounds.

"Go out the back, if you want to live," Langston spat.

Stone didn't have to be told twice. He disappeared as the former detective drew his gun.

———

As his soldiers encircled the Sterling estate, Dinwittie was relayed an urgent message from the mayor's office: The FBI was to handle the Caprice arrest. Agents would be there at any moment. Do not proceed.

The colonel was enraged.

He'd been denied his moment of glory, not once but several times: when the barricade proved to be unmanned; when the school went unguarded; and when the terrorists in the field calmly surrendered *en masse.*

But now he had the ringleader surrounded, and nobody was going to take that away from him. Especially not some weak-kneed mayor.

He gave the order to take the mansion by whatever means necessary.

"But … but sir," the young captain said, sputtering. "The directive from the mayor?"

"What directive?" the commander replied.

From across the treed boulevard, Dinwittie watched as a squad of soldiers approached the entrance to the sprawling home.

"You have a green light," the colonel said into his walkie-talkie.

The squad split into two, taking up positions on either side of the doors. Finding them unlocked, they carefully pushed them in.

The first two soldiers came under fire the moment they entered. Both were wounded and howled in pain.

Dinwittie, stunned, yelled at the soldiers positioned on the lawn to attack. Within seconds, a dozen of them began storming the house.

"Kill them!" the commander shouted. "Kill them all!"

———

Langston always figured it would end like this. Violently, fatally, in a furious eruption of blood and bone.

With Father's help, he'd risen above his frailties, banished his suicidal thoughts. Thanks to the teachings of People's Oasis, Langston had become a better man – or at least a man with a purpose.

And at this moment, his purpose was to buy Father the time he needed to complete his holy work. While parts of God's plan, administered through the reverend, were admittedly beyond his comprehension, he trusted Father like none other.

When he spotted the advancing soldiers, Langston created a defensive wall less than 15 feet from the door by flipping over a pair of heavy oak console tables. Crouching behind then, he waited patiently. When the doors swung open, he squeezed the trigger.

He was smiling when the first two went down, followed by two more, all screaming in agony.

Langston could see from their faces that the part-time soldiers were young, likely early 20s, and that fact bothered him a little. But there was nothing he could do. No alternative, other than to buy precious time and serve God's will.

When the smoke bomb hit the floor, he laughed. He'd just have to be a bit more patient. Wait for them to get within an arm's length.

When a soldier suddenly materialized in the fog, Langston said, "Hello." He clubbed the man in the face with his gun.

Two more soldiers went down, with fierce punches, before the others retreated back outside.

Minutes later, a grenade rolled up to the barrier. Then a second. Then a third.

Langston watched in a detached sort of way.

Just before the explosions, he looked up, as if to heaven, and yelled.

"For you, Father!"

———

Fallone raced up the stairs two at a time.

Moments earlier, he had carefully approached the advancing soldiers, waving a white pillowcase. From the front porch, he explained that he was the security chief for the estate. There was nobody but the owner inside, but they were welcome to search.

When they lowered their rifles and moved on, he let out a deep breath.

The safe room was hidden in an upstairs library that doubled as a reading refuge. Still catching his breath, he pressed the button that unlocked a hinged bookcase and pushed it open.

Rapping hard on the reinforced door with his knuckles, he stared into the peephole.

"Cicely, it's me!"

She opened the door and collapsed in his thick arms.

"You're safe," he said as they slowly pulled apart. "You're safe now."

Weathers studied his soft eyes, saw his love. *Did she feel the same?*

She wasn't the same woman she was a couple of weeks ago. She'd changed, possibly in profound ways. She'd need time to process her feelings, assess the powerful emotions crashing like ocean waves inside her.

Absently, she twisted the gold band on her finger.

"We should talk," she told him.

THIRTY-SIX

THE FBI ARRIVED moments after the bloody shootout and immediately took over.

The first action was to order everyone affiliated with the National Guard to leave the island.

Smythe, the senior FBI agent, stormed over to Dinwittie. Wounded soldiers were being removed on stretchers. Black smoke from the grenades was still rising from the front of the mansion.

"You SOB, I'll have you court-martialed for this," Smythe hollered at the commander. "Directly disobeying orders. *Grenades?* Are you effing kidding me?"

For once, Dinwittie had nothing to say. No sharp retort. He just looked sad and confused.

"Get this fool out of my sight," Smythe said. "We have a search to organize."

Within minutes, a handful of federal agents and a SWAT team began scouring every centimeter of the mansion and its eight-acre grounds.

They found Sterling, bound and gagged, on the kitchen floor. They found two very large dogs. And they found the billionaire's estranged wife on her favorite chaise lounge, calmly reading a paperback novel and sipping a mocktail through a straw, as if nothing at all had happened.

But they couldn't find Caprice.

When Sterling led the agents to the safe room, he shrieked. All of his treasure was gone.

"I've been robbed!" he shouted. "Everything is lost! *Everything!*"

Within minutes, a massive manhunt was underway, with scores of cops combing the small island. The FBI sent out bulletins with Caprice's picture and description far and wide. They alerted airports and other transit centers. Every roadside camera was checked and monitored.

Inside the mansion, authorities began punching holes in walls and ceilings, searching for potential hiding places. They opened up ventilation shafts. Put miniature scanning devices up every vent and all six chimneys. They even used high-tech thermal imaging gear, searching for body heat.

But after several hours, they gave a collective shrug.

The priest was nowhere to be found.

Sterling was sitting cross-legged on the floor of the safe room, morose and mourning his loss, when he suddenly had an idea.

"The hatch!" he cried.

Smythe dashed into the room to find Sterling pulling up the commercial-grade carpeting in a corner of the room. Below was a door with recessed hinges. He pulled it open, exposing a ladder descending into a concrete tunnel.

"What the fuck is this?" Smythe demanded.

"Escape hatch," Sterling said, brightening. "In case things get really bad."

"Where does it lead?"

"Under the house, to a cave by the shore. There's a pair of

WaveRunners down there."

"That's how he got out!"

The agent pulled his gun and motioned for several SWAT officers to follow. They scrambled down the ladder, Sterling a safe distance behind.

When the tunnel opened into the cave, the officers had their assault weapons pointed and ready. But the natural hollow was empty. The WaveRunners hadn't been touched.

Smythe swept the cave with his flashlight but saw nothing. The air was thick with humidity. The sound of cops walking on the floor of hard-packed dirt and rock echoed like drumbeats.

"Some kind of vanishing act," the FBI man muttered.

None of the other cult leaders he'd studied would do such a thing: Disappear. For them, it was all about ego, about maintaining control to the end.

"It's four miles to the mainland," Sterling said, trying to be helpful. "Could he have tried swimming?"

"Have you tried swimming with more than a hundred pounds of loot?" the agent replied frostily. "Besides, a web of police boats is out there. Nobody can get through."

With any luck, Caprice had taken his own life at the water's edge. Then Smythe could put a bow on the case and move on. Nice and neat.

"Get divers in the water to look for a body," he told the other agents. "*Immediately!*"

———

Relieved that his daily TV standups were over, Stone banged out a vivid account of the last day of the Turner Island standoff and filed it to Betters.

While other members of the press had finally made it onto the island, the Chronicle still had an exclusive – at least for one more news cycle.

Nobody but Stone could recount what went down that day with more detail and human emotion, because he alone was there. It was a gripping tale with compelling characters and a mysterious ending. And it was all true. There was just one part of the story he chose not to include.

"Some of your best work, Jeremy," Betters said after finishing the edit. "Great to have you back."

"Thanks, Sally. Thanks for always being there for me."

"Are you coming in tomorrow?"

"Yeah, a lot of threads to follow. Lots of angles."

"We'll talk about it later. Try to get some sleep."

Sleep. Stone wondered when the last time was that he got a full night's rest. Not since before his wife's diagnosis, he reckoned.

He gathered up his things and thanked the kind doctor for the use of his home. Then he walked through the business district, accepting handshakes from the relieved residents, as he headed to his car.

Weathers caught up to him.

"Jeremy, I suppose I should thank you," she said.

"What for?"

"Telling the world what happened here. In the middle of a siege. That took courage."

"Not really. That's all I know how to do."

"So, what are you going to do now?"

Stone gave a tight smile.

"Some more writing," he said. "I miss it."

THIRTY-SEVEN

ANOTHER FITFUL night. Another guest appearance by the ghost of Daniels, demanding answers.

"Leave me alone!"

Stone tossed the sheets and swung his legs over the edge of the bed. He clicked on a lamp and the apparition disappeared. Checking his phone, he groaned. It was 4:15. Even the sun had the good sense not to be up that early.

His head was throbbing in a different way. He'd been sober for a while now, having resisted the lure of the island booze closet, and it felt both good and bad.

He longed for a soothing drink, could still taste the liquor in the back of his throat, smooth and hot. And yet without question his newfound sobriety had helped revive a flagging career. Rescued it, actually.

Stone was now working on a book – billed as "the true inside story of the Turner Island standoff" – that came with a staggering $750,000 advance.

The manuscript was about half written, but already he was dreading the ending. Could it really be a true story if he withheld the full truth about what happened? And if he did reveal what actually went down in the safe room, would Caprice, wherever he was, make good on his threat?

Stone wondered darkly if his publisher would print a book written by an author accused of crushing a man to death with a car. An author sent to prison.

Opening the side drawer of his desk, he found the blackmail envelope he'd buried under printouts. He opened the clasp and removed the photo.

There it was: The car in the middle of the road. The body lying by the front tires. Daniels' lifeless face, captured in black and white.

Why am I torturing myself? I should burn it. Never look at it again.

He pushed his laptop out of the way and slumped onto the top of the desk, head resting on his arms. He stayed there, motionless, for a long while. Then an idea wormed its way into his brain. Something in the photo that had caught his eye.

Slowly, he lifted his head and forced himself to take another look. The darkness around the body was different than the darkness around the car. It was subtle, yes, but different – as if one half was shot in moonlight and the other on a cloudy night.

Stone fished around the drawer until he found an old gift, a combination magnifying glass and letter opener. He examined the photo again, using the glass.

"Holy shit," he whispered.

There was something wrong with the image, something manufactured. But he'd need to be sure. Fortunately, the expert he needed was close at hand.

A few hours later, he was at the Chronicle consulting with veteran photographer Karl Svendsen. He'd worked with Stone on many top stories, developing a close friendship, a bond that had been battle-tested by the reporter's destructive binge drinking.

Stone showed him the photo and Svendsen immediately put it under his high-powered, illuminated magnifier.

"It's a fake," he pronounced after a few minutes. "See the seam? It's been altered digitally."

"You mean, like, Photoshopped?"

"There's lots of software tools out there, but yeah." He handed Stone back the photo. "Not a bad job of fusing images. Would fool the eye – if you don't look too close."

Stone took a deep breath. He looked relieved.

"Thanks, man. I owe you one," he said, patting the photographer on the back.

"Hey, what's this all abou—?" Svendsen began, but Stone had already hustled off.

—

McHenry had his own demons to exorcise.

His decision to frame Stone for the killing of the old man had proved to be more troubling than he'd thought.

The photograph he'd altered delighted Langston – as much as Langston was capable of being delighted, anyway. He and the preacher had the leverage they wanted to make the reporter do their bidding.

McHenry was paid double his usual fee, which should have ended things. But he'd put a man into a ditch. He'd taken a life and such matters were never neatly disposed of.

It wasn't until after the standoff that he realized the scope of the bodacious plan executed by Caprice. Whether it was cover for a brilliant heist or an elaborate political stunt not seen since the 1973 Indian occupation of Wounded Knee, South Dakota, McHenry couldn't say.

He just knew there was an opportunity in the aftermath to come clean. And maybe, just maybe, avoid time behind bars.

With a lawyer's help, he brokered a sweeping immunity deal in which he'd reveal his knowledge of the plan to recruit and control Stone as a key participant in the Turner Island takeover.

The feds, confident that Caprice would soon be in their custody facing a host of charges, eagerly questioned McHenry for hours. He gave them honest answers, detailing how he surveilled the reporter, took the incriminating photo and more. He shared every word that Langston had told him, although admittedly there weren't very many.

And, in the end, when his immunity was guaranteed, he calmly revealed that he was the one who ran down Daniels on a foggy night.

He explained, in full detail, how he doctored the photo, splicing two images together in his bathroom darkroom.

Everyone in the room looked shocked, even his lawyer. But McHenry smiled, knowing he'd sleep better.

A deal was a deal.

———

At the launch site in the desert, Sterling and his A-list celebrity guests were ready to party.

The massive unmanned Galactix rocket, bound for Mars, was on the pad, pointed at the heavens. As the countdown commenced, the billionaire couldn't hide his excitement. Everything in his life paled compared to this moment – his moment of triumph.

"Eight ... seven ... six ..."

The rocket program had cost him dearly, but it was about to pay off. NASA, the Chinese, the Russians. They'd all be investing heavily in his company very, very soon.

"Five ... four ... three..."

Sterling was already accepting pats on the back. He wondered what he'd say when the president called to offer congratulations.

"Two ... one ... liftoff!"

From the safety of the viewing platform, Sterling watched in awe as the rocket launched atop a fireball, rising into the atmosphere. Everyone cheered. A galvanized bucket with six bottles of French champagne on ice was brought into the room.

Exactly 22 seconds later, Galactix Explorer V exploded.

CHAPTER
THIRTY-EIGHT

HE CAME FROM the sea on a crisp autumn morning.

Swinging one flippered foot after the other, he pulled himself onto the stone ledge. It was cold and slick, dampened by the waves.

The diver shed his flippers and tank, then paused to examine the his-and-her WaveRunners, still offering an escape. He wouldn't need them. His boat was waiting a quarter-mile offshore and what he had to move would be much lighter underwater.

He stepped deeper into the cave, entering the shadows.

Searching for the spot with his hands, he unearthed the small spade he'd hidden under some rocky dirt. Then he dug until he found the treasure, buried a foot below.

The diver swept the dirt off the bulging nylon bag and filled in the hole, packing it down with his feet. He dragged the heavy satchel across the cave. It made a loud scraping noise against the rock, but he was alone and no one could hear.

He was tempted to sneak a peek at what glimmered within. A quick pull of the zipper was all it would take.

Instead, he smiled and slipped back into his flippers. He buckled on the tank. Stepping to the water's edge, he lifted the bag, using both arms.

With a splash, he was gone.

This time, for good.

———

People's Oasis closed in dramatic fashion, with bright yellow police tape across the front door.

While the fruitless manhunt dragged on, the Justice Department and IRS took aim at the church, stripping away its tax-exempt status and investigating every real and imagined link to the situation on Turner Island. A U.S. Senate committee subpoenaed Caprice in absentia, demanding that he appear in Washington, D.C., to answer questions about his "brazen acts of domestic terrorism."

But among the have-nots, Caprice's legend as the ultimate Robin Hood grew.

A few days before the takeover, Caprice had tapped the church's coffers, giving everyone in the tent city several thousand dollars. Enough for a fresh start.

Joseph, the veteran, bought himself a used camper and began traveling the country. But when the standoff ended and the reverend vanished, he returned to the familiar sidewalk in front of the shuttered church.

He hung a sign on the chain-link fence. HE LIVES, it read.

At night, around burn barrels in cities across the country, tales were told of Caprice's cunning and fearlessness. Some of them were even true.

In Hollywood, movie scripts were being penned, although one

major studio had already locked up the rights to Stone's upcoming book. Timothy Chalamet had reportedly been offered the priestly starring role. A TV mini series and a Netflix documentary were also in the works.

On Turner Island, shopkeepers grumbled only to themselves. There had been no mass conversion to the cause, just a desire to cash in.

Stores began selling T-shirts emblazoned with Caprice's Jesus-like image. A company started giving guided tours of standoff-related sites, including Billionaire's Row, Turner Academy and the stone bench "where he heard God's word." A café named a club sandwich after the preacher, featuring "holy" Swiss cheese.

Tourists from around the world flocked to the scene, which had taken on a quasi-religious significance. Weathers' Airbnb was now booked solid two years in advance. A petition was circulating to allow the island's first boutique hotels, citing "incredible demand." A mural depicting the standoff was commissioned.

What went unnoticed in all the hubbub was the money.

It never stopped coming.

Anonymous deposits in the bank accounts of far-flung nonprofits, both big and small, seemingly at random intervals. Not huge amounts of funds that would draw scrutiny, but enough to keep certain programs running.

If somebody was to dig into it, they'd discover that the deposits totaled millions and originated from a complex web of offshore accounts that were virtually impossible to trace.

There would be no more announcements, no press releases or fanfare of any kind, by either the donor or the recipients.

Paid staffers and volunteers would simply gather around and smile in a goofy way, like best friends sharing a sweet secret.

Some would whisper two words:

He lives.

CHAPTER

THIRTY-NINE

STONE'S BOOK became an instant bestseller, selling out the first printing in a few weeks.

Even literary critics liked it, with one calling "Island of the Rich" a "powerful and often profound debut."

Stone had been granted a six-month leave to write the 336-page true story, following a promise to Burgess that the Chronicle could be the first to publish an excerpt. He delivered the manuscript a couple of weeks early, a feat he attributed to both the drama of the story and his ongoing sobriety.

For the first time, the world read about Caprice loading up a duffel bag with diamonds and gold as authorities closed in. But that shocking scene was tempered by Stone's conversations with the directors of many worthy nonprofits who had benefited from the billion-dollar fund.

For them, the priest was a hero of the highest order.

Stone supposed it helped book sales that Caprice remained at large, a wanted man. Fallone had revealed to the FBI that he saw scuba gear in the bed of the truck, which led to speculation that the priest had made his escape underwater, swimming right under the police boats.

On his book promotion tour, the first question interviewers often asked the author was "Where do you think he is?"

"I have no idea if he's alive or dead. It's a real mystery, isn't it?" Stone would answer with an impish grin, although that was only partially true.

He'd gotten wind of the continuing windfall propping up nonprofits while researching his book. Not only was Caprice alive, he appeared to be carrying on his work while on the lam, operating out of his own Sherwood Forest.

Stone kept that shiny nugget to himself, like a wintering squirrel gathers nuts. Or, in this case, fodder for a possible sequel.

Outwardly, the journalist seemed embarrassed by his sudden fame, especially the action figure with the notebook accessory, but the truth was he enjoyed the attention.

Newspaper stories, no matter how big and meaningful, never drew mobs of autograph-seeking fans, international press conferences, appearances on daytime TV talk shows and paparazzi. At the Chronicle, after a blockbuster story hit the stands, there was just self-satisfaction and a boss with pages to fill, saying, "Good job, what's next?"

There was something about the Turner Island standoff, though, that captured the imagination of millions of people. They were now hanging on Stone's every word, as if he was some guru chock full of wisdom.

Seeking more candid personal moments, a cluster of photographers would follow him home and camp in their cars overnight. They knew his favorite restaurants and main courses, learned what coffee drink he ordered every morning. The more personal the info, it seemed, the better.

"Do you have a girlfriend?" they would shout.

Usually, Stone just shrugged and kept walking. But one morning, out of frustration, he blurted out the name of his favorite movie actress – Ingrid Helvig, a young Scandinavian beauty.

After that tidbit actually made the tabloids, Stone laughed. The joke was on them. *Preposterous.*

The next day, he met with his literary agent to go over some more planned appearances. She told him Helvig's rep had called.

Would he be interested in meeting the actress? Maybe grabbing dinner?

Yeah, Stone's life was like that.

Finally.

———

The postcard arrived at the Tudor Arms on the anniversary of the island invasion.

It featured an underwater picture. A rainbow of tropical fish and an equally colorful coral reef. The location wasn't listed.

The message read:

My dear friend: It pleases me that you are doing well. And to think it all began with the promise of a scoop. Is that the right word?

It was signed, "Robin Hood."

AUTHOR'S NOTE

The Have-Nots is my fourth novel, and in some ways the most personally revealing.

The character at the heart of the tale, Jeremy Stone, is drawn from my experiences as an investigative journalist. At least the outer boundaries. The relentless pursuit of truth. The tough, confrontational interviews. The pressure to perform under the searing heat of deadlines, always counting down.

But that's where the parallels end. Stone is a troubled soul, a recovering alcoholic, making him the perfect pawn for a cunning radical priest. When I was a reporter, there were many long days and nights, and a fair amount of booze, but nothing close to Stone's level of abuse, agony and self-torment.

Still, I could relate to the character rising to the challenge of covering the world's biggest news story from the inside.

Readers will no doubt ask what inspired this book, and I'd have to say it started with Bernie Sanders.

The senator from Vermont has long called for the nation's billionaires to pay their fair share and help lift up the less fortunate. Since his quixotic crusade began, however, the rich have only gotten richer and the divide between wealthy and poor become a vast chasm.

The best of Sanders' many speeches railing against the One Percenters helped frame the sermon in *The Have-Nots*, as delivered by the priest, Charles Caprice.

The widening divide between the haves and have-nots in the

world made me think. What if an island inhabited by billionaires was stormed by radicals bent on playing Robin Hood?

Well, now you know how such an invasion might play out, at least in one writer's imagination.

There are many people to thank for helping bring *The Have-Nots* to fruition.

I am deeply appreciative of my great friend, East Coast journalist Bridget Murphy, for her insight on matters of plotting and character development, among many other things.

Another talented journalist, Ann Butler, went above and beyond in her critiques and line editing. Jesse Miller, Jim Floyd, Naomi Mahncke and Bonnie Ross offered invaluable feedback after reading drafts, and too many others to name provided the kind of encouragement that keeps the creative fires burning.

I want to thank the fine people of Astoria, Oregon, and the North Coast for their amazing support, buying my books and attending author fairs, readings and the like.

Independent authors such as myself simply couldn't exist without equally devoted readers. Thanks for joining me on this journey.

W.D.

ALSO BY WILLIAM DEAN

DANGEROUS FREEDOM

"I'M FREE and I don't know how to act," Bud Baker says after he's roused from his prison cell and seated on a bus in the middle of the night. He aims to make his way to Alaska, where he has a cabin and childhood memories, but he lingers in a sleepy Oregon town after falling for the beautiful Jo Jo Summers. She tells him the tragic story of an addict whose baby was stolen at birth. When she asks Bud to return the boy to his birth mother, he refuses – until she reveals that the woman is her sister. Bud risks his newfound freedom by reverting to his criminal ways, expecting a manhunt. But he's already being hunted – by demons from his past.

290 pages. Available on Amazon and in bookstores.

———

THE **GHOSTS** WE **KNOW**

SUNNY SLOPE was long touted as northern Oregon's "friendliest neighborhood." But that was before a predator moved in. A young teenage boy took his own life. Another suddenly disappeared without a trace. As fear took hold of the community, the playground at its heart suddenly deserted, Harry Bolden and Fred Von Stiller knew they had to do something. The aging veterans launched an investigation of their own – only to find themselves in the crosshairs of a sinister organization. *The Ghosts We Know* is the harrowing yet heartwarming story of an unlikely friendship forged in the fires of a community under siege.

298 pages. Available on Amazon and in bookstores.

—

MILITIA MEN

IN A COASTAL Oregon town, best friends Robb and Sean are often found rooted in their couch, smoking pot and playing video games. Then one night they cross paths with True Patriots and everything changes. Sean finds himself under the spell of the militia's charismatic yet delusional leader, an ex-Marine called Viper. Robb reluctantly joins in hopes of protecting Sean only to become embroiled in a plot to kidnap U.S. Sen. Alexandra Austin, a mass shooting survivor whose landmark gun control bill has drawn the ire of far-right extremists. When the plot turns real, Robb desperately searches for a way out. Will it be too late?

274 pages. Available on Amazon and in bookstores.

ABOUT THE AUTHOR

WILLIAM DEAN is a former investigative journalist who left newspaper work to pursue a second career as a novelist. He is the author of three engrossing tales of suspense, all set amid the misty forests of the Pacific Northwest: *Militia Men*, *The Ghosts We Know* and *Dangerous Freedom*. He lives in Astoria, Oregon, where he also writes and blogs about craft beer.

FIND HIM ONLINE AT:
WILLIAMDEANBOOKS.COM